When Eustacia saw Clym's face in the mirror, she froze. His face was ashy, haggard, and terrible. She paled.

"You know what I'm thinking, don't you?" he said huskily. "I can see it in your face."

She didn't speak.

"Answer me," he ordered. "Did you keep our door shut against my mother the day that she died?"

Eustacia remained silent.

Clym grabbed her by the arm.

"What are you going to do?" she asked with some defiance. "You don't frighten me."

Instead of letting go, Clym pulled her closer. "Tell me about my mother's death," he said in a hard, panting whisper, "or I'll . . ."

A Background Note about
The Return of the Native

The Return of the Native takes place in south-west England in the 1850s, when socioeconomic status was all-important. People rarely married someone of another social class. Members of the upper class felt considerable snobbery, even contempt, for those of lower classes. And members of lower classes felt respect, even awe, for their social "betters."

In *The Return of the Native*, Thomas Hardy shows how rigid class distinctions contributed to unhappiness, especially by interfering with romantic love. For example, Diggory Venn loves Tamsin Yeobright but belongs to a lower social class. Much of the book's tension arises from class barriers, which are part of a world (in Hardy's view) where randomness and chance are key parts of everyday life.

THE RETURN OF THE
NATIVE

THOMAS HARDY

Edited, and with an Afterword,
by Joan Dunayer

 THE TOWNSEND LIBRARY

THE RETURN OF THE NATIVE

TP **THE TOWNSEND LIBRARY**

For more titles in the Townsend Library,
visit our website: **www.townsendpress.com**

All new material in this edition is
copyright © 2005 by Townsend Press.
Printed in the United States of America

0 9 8 7 6 5 4 3 2 1

Townsend Press, Inc.
1038 Industrial Drive
West Berlin, New Jersey 08091

ISBN 1-59194-044-3

Library of Congress Control Number:
2004118013

CONTENTS

AFTERWORD

CHAPTER 1

Egdon Heath, a vast tract of uncultivated land in the county of Dorset, England, was untamable. Covered with ferns and low shrubs, it was majestic, but not severe, in its monotony. The storm was its lover and the wind its friend. Ever since the beginning of vegetation, its soil had worn the same brown dress. The place had an ancient permanence. The sea changed; the fields changed; the rivers, villages, and people changed. But Egdon Heath remained the same.

At twilight on Guy Fawkes Day*, 1850, Egdon Heath was darkening. The cloudy sky was a vast white tent. As other things sank to sleep, the heath slowly awakened and listened.

Captain Vye, a retired naval officer, walked along the road that crossed the heath. White-haired and slightly stooped, he wore a faded hat

*Guy Fawkes Day, on November 5, is an annual British holiday. On this day, Britons celebrate the failure of a 1605 plot by Guy Fawkes and others to blow up the British parliament. In the mid-19th century, the day commonly was celebrated with evening bonfires.

and cloak. The image of an anchor decorated each of his brass buttons. He used a silver-headed walking stick as a third leg. Every few inches, he poked the ground with its point. The long road stretched before him: dry, empty, and white. It divided the vast, dark heath like the part on a head of black hair. Vye frequently looked ahead to see how much farther he had to go. After a time, he saw a wagon some distance in front of him. It moved slowly, so he gained on it.

Diggory Venn walked beside the wagon, which was red. His cap, boots, face, hands—all were red. He was a ruddleman, whose job was to supply ruddle, a bright red iron ore, dug from pits, with which farmers marked their sheep.

Vye came up alongside Diggory. "Good evening."

Diggory turned his head. "Good evening." He was twenty-four years old, tall and slim, with an attractive, clean-shaven face. His blue eyes were as keen as a bird of prey's. He wore a fitted, high-quality corduroy suit and had a dignified manner.

Apart from his greeting, Diggory showed no desire to talk, although he continued to walk alongside Vye. There were no sounds except the wind on the vegetation, the wagon's wheels, and the footsteps of Diggory, Vye, and the two shaggy ponies—small and hardy—who drew the wagon.

Periodically Diggory would leave Vye's side and, stepping behind the wagon, anxiously look inside through a small window. Then he'd return to

Vye. Neither man found the silence awkward. In lonely places, travelers frequently greet each other and then plod on for miles without talking. The two men might not have spoken again until their parting had it not been for Diggory's visits to his wagon. After he looked in a fifth time, Vye asked, "Is something inside there besides your load?"

"Yes."

"Someone who needs looking after?"

"Yes."

A faint cry came from inside the wagon. Diggory hastened to the back, looked in, and came away again.

"Do you have a child there?"

"No, sir, a woman."

"Why did she cry out?"

"She's fallen asleep and, not being used to traveling, she's uneasy and keeps dreaming."

"A young woman?"

"Yes."

"Is she your wife?"

"No," Diggory said bitterly. "She's above mating with the likes of me. But there's no reason why I should tell you about that."

"That's true. And there's no reason why you shouldn't."

Diggory looked into Vye's face. "Well, sir," he said, "I knew her before today, although perhaps it would have been better if I hadn't. I'm nothing to her. She wouldn't be in my wagon if a better vehicle had been there to take her."

"Been where?"

"Anglebury."

"I know the town well. What was she doing there?"

"Not much. She's tired now and unwell. That's what makes her so restless. She dropped off into a nap about an hour ago. It'll do her good."

"Is she a good-looking woman?"

"Yes."

Vye turned his eyes toward the wagon window. "May I look at her?"

"No," Diggory said sharply. "I have no right to allow you that. I hope she won't wake up until she's home."

"Who is she? Someone from this neighborhood? Is she that Blooms End woman who's been talked about lately? If so, I know her, and I can guess what's happened."

"It's of no matter. You and I soon will have to part company. My ponies are tired, and I have farther to go. I'm going to rest them under this bank for an hour."

Vye nodded indifferently, and Diggory turned his horses and wagon in on the turf. "Good night."

"Good night," Vye returned, and he went on his way.

Diggory watched his form as it shrank to a speck on the road and disappeared into the night. He took some hay from a metal frame under the wagon and, throwing some of it in front of the horses, used the rest to make a pad that he laid on the ground beside the wagon. He sat on the pad, leaning his back against the wheel. He heard a low, soft breathing from inside the wagon.

Diggory looked around. He spotted a barrow, a large mound of earth built up over an ancient burial site. Known as Rainbarrow, the mound was the heath's highest part.

A woman stood on the mound. She shifted a step or two and turned around. Apparently alarmed, she descended on the mound's right side, like a water drop gliding down a bud, and vanished.

The reason for her sudden departure now appeared. As she dropped out of sight on the mound's right side, other people climbed the mound's left side. Soon the mound was covered with people, silhouettes against the sky. Each deposited a load of gorse branches, bound together, on top of the mound.

A pyramid of gorse thirty feet around now occupied the mound's crown. The landscape began to change. One by one, bonfires appeared, flecking the countryside. Some were distant. Others were large and near. About thirty could be counted within the district.

The first tall flame from Rainbarrow sprang into the sky. The cheerful blaze lit the men and women who stood on the mound.

"Tamsin Yeobright and Damon Wildeve went to Anglebury this morning to get married,"

Timothy Fairway said. "They must have returned to the Quiet Woman Inn by now."

"Last fall Mrs. Yeobright forbade the marriage, but then she changed her mind," Humphrey Miller the gorse-cutter said. He was a somewhat solemn young fellow. "I guess they married in Anglebury because marrying here would have embarrassed Mrs. Yeobright."

"A lady like Tamsin must have disliked being married without a proper wedding," Susan Nunsuch said. "I don't know what she sees in Damon Wildeve, although some may say that he's good-looking."

"Wildeve's a clever, educated fellow, almost as clever as Clym Yeobright," Timothy said.

"Yes, Clym's wonderfully smart," Humphrey said. "I saw Mrs. Yeobright last night. She said that he'll be coming home at Christmas."

"He should have come before and married Tamsin himself," Susan said.

"Maybe he's just coming to spend some time with Mrs. Yeobright. She'll be feeling lonely now that Tamsin has left Blooms End," Humphrey said.

The bonfire was beginning to dwindle, as were most of the other fires within the wide horizon. One fire, about a mile off, continued to burn bright. "I think that bonfire's at Captain Vye's," Timothy said.

"Vye's granddaughter is a strange one," Susan said. "She keeps to herself."

"She's attractive," Humphrey said, "especially when she's wearing one of her best dresses."

"We'd better be getting home," Timothy said. The fire now was nothing more than a circle of ashes flecked with red embers and sparks.

"Hoi!" Diggory called from the darkness.

"Halloo!" Timothy called back.

"Is there a wagon road up across here to Mrs. Yeobright's?" Diggory asked as he climbed the barrow, having left his wagon below.

"Yes," Timothy said. "Keep along the path down there."

"I mean a road that two horses and a wagon can travel over?"

"Yes. It will take you to the valley below. The road's a bit rough, but if you've got a light, your horses will find their way."

"Thank you. Good night." Diggory headed back down the barrow.

"I think I've seen him before," Humphrey said.

Elizabeth Yeobright now approached. She was a well-respected, genteel widow. She was middle-aged, thin, with strong features that suggested intelligence, character, and aloofness. Her husband had been a farmer and her father a clergyman.

"Mrs. Yeobright, a few minutes ago a young ruddleman was here asking the way to your house," Sam Brown the turf-cutter said.

"What did he want?" she asked.

"He didn't say. I'm glad to hear that Mr. Clym is coming home at Christmas, ma'am," Sam said.

"Yes," she said.

"He must be a fine fellow now," Timothy said.

"He's a man now," Elizabeth said quietly. "I must go now. I'm headed to the inn. Tamsin is returning there tonight with her husband. Will you walk with me, Olivia?"

"Surely, ma'am," Olivia Dowden the broom-maker answered.

"You'll probably encounter the ruddleman that I mentioned," Timothy said. "He just went back to his wagon. We heard that your niece and her husband were coming home as soon as they were married. We're going to the inn soon to congratulate them."

"Thank you," Elizabeth said. "Are you ready, Olivia?"

"Yes, ma'am. There's a light shining from the inn. It will guide us." Olivia indicated a faint light at the bottom of the valley, and the two women descended the barrow.

CHAPTER 2

"So Tamsin has married Mr. Wildeve at last," Olivia said.

"Yes."

"I guess you'll miss her. She's like a daughter to you."

"Yes."

"I was surprised to hear that you agreed to the wedding, ma'am."

"You weren't more surprised than I myself would have been a year ago. There are many sides to that wedding. I couldn't tell you all of them even if I tried."

"I felt that Mr. Wildeve wasn't solid enough to marry into your family. After all, he keeps an inn. Still, he seems clever. They say that he used to be an engineer and a gentleman but he's come down in the world."

"I decided that, on the whole, it would be best if Tamsin married the man of her choice."

"Poor little thing. No doubt, her feelings got the better of her. Well, people may say what they

9

will, but Mr. Wildeve has several acres of property in addition to the inn, and his manners are gentlemanly. Besides, what's done can't be undone."

"No, it can't," Elizabeth said. "Here's the wagon track. We can follow it."

They soon reached a diverging path. Olivia turned to the left toward her house, and Elizabeth continued straight ahead.

When Elizabeth was about to enter the inn, she saw a horse and wagon coming toward her. Holding a lantern, Diggory walked alongside.

Elizabeth walked toward the wagon. "I think you've been asking for me," she said. "I'm Mrs. Yeobright of Blooms End."

Diggory stopped the horses and gestured to Elizabeth to step aside with him. "You don't know me, ma'am?"

"No," she said. "Why, yes, I do! You're young Venn. Your father was a dairyman."

"Yes. I knew your niece, Miss Tamsin, a little. She's inside my wagon."

"What?" Elizabeth said, alarmed.

"I can't explain much, ma'am. I was going along the road this morning, about a mile from Anglebury, when I heard something trotting after me like a doe. I looked around and there she was, white as death. She said, 'Oh, Diggory, I thought it was you. Will you help me? I'm in trouble.'"

"How does she come to call you by your first name?"

"I knew her before I became a ruddleman.

She asked me if she could ride, and she fainted. I picked her up and put her inside. She's been there ever since. She's cried a lot, but she's hardly spoken. She told me only that she was supposed to get married this morning. I tried to get her to eat something, but she wouldn't. Finally, she fell asleep."

"Let me see her," Elizabeth said, hurrying toward the wagon.

Diggory followed with the lantern and, stepping up first, helped Elizabeth mount beside him. When the wagon's door was opened, she saw a makeshift couch at the other end. Diggory had hung drapes around the couch, to prevent the red materials of his trade from touching Tamsin, who lay there covered with a cloak. She was asleep.

The lantern's light fell on her features. Her face was pale but sweet, honest, and pretty. She had full, wavy light-brown hair. Opening her eyes, she cried, "Oh, Aunt!"

"Tamsin!" Elizabeth stooped over Tamsin and kissed her.

Panting lightly, Tamsin sat upright. "Where am I?"

"Nearly home, my dear. In Egdon Bottom. This kind man, who has done so much, will take you on to Blooms End." Elizabeth turned to Diggory, who had withdrawn from the front of the wagon when Tamsin awoke.

"Of course I will," he said.

"He's very kind," Tamsin murmured. "I was

once acquainted with him. When I saw him today, I thought that I'd rather be in his wagon than the vehicle of some stranger. But I'll walk now."

Aunt and niece descended from the wagon. "Didn't your father leave you his dairy farm?" Elizabeth asked Diggory.

"Yes, ma'am."

"Then, why did you become a ruddleman?"

Diggory looked at Tamsin, who blushed. "You won't be needing me any more tonight, ma'am?"

"I think not, since Tamsin wishes to walk. We'll soon be up the path and home. Thank you."

Diggory moved on with his wagon, and the two women remained standing in the road. As soon as Diggory was out of hearing, Elizabeth turned to her niece and said sternly, "Now, Tamsin, what's the meaning of this disgraceful situation?"

Tamsin was dismayed. "I'm not married," she replied faintly. "When we got there, the minister wouldn't marry us because of a problem with the marriage license."

"What problem?"

"I don't know. Damon can explain." Tamsin wept silently.

"From the very first, when you began to feel foolish about that man, I warned you that he wouldn't make you happy. I felt it so strongly that

I did what I never would have believed myself capable of doing: I stood up in church and forbade the marriage. It's made me the stuff of gossip for weeks. But now you *have* to marry him."

"I don't wish to do otherwise. He says that we can marry in a day or two."

"I wish he'd never seen you. I'm going to the inn to see if he's returned. I'll get to the bottom of this at once. Wildeve mustn't think that he can play tricks on me or my family."

"It wasn't a trick. The license was wrong, and he couldn't get another the same day."

"Why didn't *he* bring you back?"

"That was my doing," Tamsin said. "When I found out that we couldn't marry, I didn't want to come back with him. I felt ill. Then I saw Diggory and was glad to get him to take me home. I can't explain it any better."

They turned toward the Quiet Woman Inn, which faced the heath and Rainbarrow. "He seems to be home," Elizabeth said.

"Must I come in, Aunt?"

"Yes, so that he doesn't lie to me. We won't stay more than a few minutes."

The women entered the inn. Elizabeth tapped at the door of the private parlor, unfastened it, and looked in. Damon Wildeve was sitting in front of the fire. He turned, rose, and came toward his visitors. He was a young, graceful, slender man with a thick head of hair.

"Tamsin, you've reached home. How could you leave me that way, darling?" Turning to Elizabeth, he said, "It was useless to argue with her. She insisted on going, and on going alone."

"What's the meaning of it all?" Elizabeth demanded haughtily.

"Take a seat," Damon said, placing chairs for the two women. "It was a stupid mistake. The license was useless at Anglebury. It was made out for Budmouth. I hadn't read it, so I wasn't aware of that. I was in Budmouth until two days ago, and I'd intended to marry Tamsin there. But when I came to fetch her, we decided on Anglebury. I forgot that a new license would be necessary. Afterward, there wasn't time to get to Budmouth."

"You're very much to blame," Elizabeth said.

"It's my fault that we chose Anglebury," Tamsin pleaded. "I proposed it because I'm not known there."

"I know that I'm to blame," Damon said shortly.

"It's a great slight to me and my family," Elizabeth said. "When it becomes known, it will be very unpleasant for us. How can Tamsin look her friends in the face tomorrow? It's a great injury and one that I can't easily forgive. It may even reflect on her character."

"Nonsense," Damon said.

During this exchange, Tamsin looked anxiously from one face to the other. "Aunt, will you allow me to discuss this alone with Damon for a few minutes? Damon?"

"Certainly, dear, if your aunt will excuse us." Damon led Tamsin into an adjoining room, leaving Elizabeth by the fire.

As soon as they were alone and the door closed, Tamsin turned her pale, tearful face to him. "Damon, I didn't mean to part from you in anger this morning. I was frightened and hardly knew what I was saying. People who don't like you whisper things that make me doubt you at times. We *are* going to marry, aren't we?"

"Of course we are. On Monday we'll go to Budmouth and marry."

"Oh, Damon, here I am asking you to marry me! By rights, you should be on your knees begging me not to refuse you and saying that it would break your heart if I did. I used to think that it would be pretty and sweet like that."

"Real life isn't like that."

"My aunt thinks so much of our family's respectability. She'll be mortified if this story gets around. So will my cousin Clym."

"Then, he'll be unreasonable. In fact, you're all rather unreasonable."

Tamsin blushed. "I don't mean to be."

Suddenly the sound of singing came from in front of the inn. "Neighbors have come to sing us a wedding welcome," Damon said.

Elizabeth burst in from the outer room.

Giving Damon an indignant look, she said, "Tamsin, here's a pretty exposure! We must leave at once."

However, it was too late to leave by the front door, where a rugged knocking had begun. Damon went to the window and came back.

Putting his hand on Elizabeth's arm, he said, "Stay here with Tamsin. I'll go out and face them. Stay here until they're gone. Sit still, and don't speak much. I'll manage them. Blundering fools!" Damon pressed Tamsin into a seat, returned to the outer room, and opened the door.

A chorus stood outside. Thomas Cantle entered the inn, nodded to Damon, and said, "Congratulations. God bless the newlyweds!"

"Thank you," Damon said with dry resentment.

A dozen others now entered. All smiled at Damon. Timothy spotted Elizabeth's bonnet through the glass partition that separated the inn's public room from the private parlor in which the women sat. "I see that Mrs. Yeobright's here."

"And I see the young bride," Thomas said, peeping in the same direction.

Damon said nothing. Producing a jar of fermented honey and water, he said, "Have some mead."

"There isn't a better drink under the sun," Thomas said.

"Cups or glasses, gentlemen?"

"If you don't mind, just pass the jar around," Thomas said. The mead circulated.

"Being married is a worthy thing, Mr. Wildeve, and the woman you've got is a diamond," Timothy said. Raising his voice so that he'd be heard through the partition, he added, "Tamsin's father was as good a fellow as ever lived. A fine singer, too."

"He's the last person you would have expected to die in the prime of life," Humphrey said.

"Well, he was sick for some months before he died," Timothy said. There was a solemn silence. Looking out the window, Timothy said, "That bonfire at Captain Vye's house is still burning." Everyone glanced out the window.

"Maybe there's some meaning in it," Christian Cantle said.

"What meaning?" Damon said sharply.

"Some people say that Eustacia Vye is a witch. In my view, she's a fine young woman, but she's always up to something odd," Timothy said.

When the jar of mead was empty, Humphrey said, "Well, I guess we'll be moving along."

Wishing Damon happiness as a married man, everyone took their leave. Damon saw them to the door.

When they were gone, Damon returned to the private parlor. The women were gone. They'd left the house through a back window. Damon laughed to himself, thought for a moment, and then put on his hat and left the inn. Outside, he looked at the bonfire at Captain Vye's house and headed toward it.

CHAPTER 3

The woman whom Diggory had seen on the barrow returned to it after the others left. She was nineteen-year-old Eustacia Vye. Tall and voluptuous, she had luxuriant black hair and dark-brown eyes with heavy lids and long lashes. Her mouth, with delicately curving lips, seemed formed for kissing.

Her native place was Budmouth, a fashionable seaside resort. Her father had been Greek, a regiment bandmaster who was a fine musician but poor. He had met his wife when she and Captain Vye, a man of good family, visited Greece. He had adopted his wife's name, made England his home, and thrived until his wife's death, after which he started drinking and soon died. Eustacia's grandfather had paid for her education, and she was left in his care.

Eustacia missed Budmouth—its military bands, gallant soldiers, and sunny seaside afternoons. She was lonely and often depressed. Her great desire was to be passionately loved.

She opened her grandfather's naval telescope and peered through it at the inn. Then she returned to the bonfire on which others had commented.

A little boy, Johnny Nunsuch, was keeping it burning. "I'm glad you've come, Miss Eustacia," he said. "I don't like being here alone."

"Nonsense. I've been gone only about twenty minutes." Her voice had a low, rich tone, like a viola. "Did anyone come while I was away?"

"Only your grandfather. He looked outdoors for you once. I told him you were walking around on the hill to look at the other bonfires."

"Good boy."

"I think I hear him coming again, Miss."

Captain Vye came into the firelight. "When are you coming indoors, Eustacia? It's almost bedtime. It's childish of you to stay outside playing with a bonfire and wasting fuel."

"I promised Johnny a good bonfire" she lied. "You go to bed, Grandfather. I'll come in soon."

Captain Vye returned to the house.

"Keep the fire burning a while longer, Johnny, and I'll give you sixpence. Put in a piece of wood every two or three minutes. I'm going to walk along the ridge a little longer, but I'll keep coming back."

Tired and sad, Johnny fed the fire as before.

Eustacia headed back toward Rainbarrow. From there, she saw Damon approaching. She hurried back to Johnny, gave him sixpence, and told him to go home.

Damon soon appeared. "I've come," he said. "I've seen your bonfire all evening, and I knew it was meant for me. You give me no peace."

"I haven't spoken with you since you deserted me for Tamsin, but today I heard that you didn't marry her after all."

"Who told you that I didn't marry her?"

"My grandfather. He took a long walk today. As he was coming home, he overtook someone who told him about a canceled wedding. I knew it must be yours."

"Does anyone else know?"

"I suppose not. It's true, isn't it? You couldn't bring yourself to marry her because you love *me*!"

"Yes, it's true. Why else would I have come?" he said with irritation.

She threw back her shawl so that the firelight shone on her face and throat. "Have you ever seen anything better than this?"

"No," he said quietly.

"Not even on Tamsin?"

"Tamsin is a pleasing, innocent woman. Let's leave her out of this."

"I felt so hopeless when I thought you'd deserted me."

"I'm sorry I caused you pain. Until I got here tonight, I intended, after this goodbye, never to see you again."

"I'm going home, then!"

"Will you see me again?"

"Only if you promise that the wedding is off because you love *me*."

"I don't think that would be good policy," Damon said, smiling. "Then you'd know the full extent of your power over me."

"Tell me."

"You already know."

"Where is Tamsin now?"

"I don't know. I prefer not to speak of her to you. I haven't married her yet. I've come in response to your call. That's enough." Damon leaned forward to kiss her.

"No," she said, moving to the other side of the fire.

"May I kiss your hand?"

"No."

"Then I wish you good night." He bowed and left.

Eustacia sighed. She knew that Damon trifled with her, but she still desired him. At times, her pride rebelled against her passion for him and she longed to be free. She put out what remained of the fire and went indoors and upstairs to bed.

Although he had started for home, Johnny had seen Eustacia with Damon. Now he came upon Diggory's wagon. He looked inside and saw Diggory sitting by a small stove. Diggory was smoking a pipe and darning a stocking. Alarmed by Diggory's all-red appearance, Johnny stumbled.

Diggory turned his lantern on Johnny. "Who are you?" he asked.

"Johnny Nunsuch, sir!"

"What are you doing here? Watching me?"

"Yes, sir. I'm going home from Miss Vye's. She had me keep up a bonfire."

"Why?"

"I don't know, but just now I saw her with a gentleman."

"What were they saying?"

"Miss Vye asked if he had called off the wedding and still loved her."

"So!"

"May I go home?"

"Yes, of course."

Johnny left, and Diggory, sitting on a stool, took a letter from a pouch. The letter was dated two years earlier:

Dear Diggory,

The question you asked me greatly surprised me. If my aunt hadn't come upon us, I would have explained why I can't marry you. I like you, but I don't feel the things that a woman should feel for the man she marries. Also, my aunt never would agree to the marriage, even if I wanted to marry you. She likes you, but she wants me to marry higher than a small dairy farmer. It's best that we not meet again. I'll always think of you as a good man and care about your well-being. I remain your faithful friend.

Tamsin Yeobright

Since the arrival of that letter, Diggory and Tamsin hadn't met until today.

Each of the next five nights, Diggory went to Rainbarrow to eavesdrop on Eustacia and Damon, but they didn't come. On the sixth night, he saw them at the barrow. He crawled near enough to overhear.

"You wish to consult me about your marriage to another woman?" Eustacia was saying indignantly. "I won't bear this any longer!" She started to cry.

"I'm in a bind," Damon said. "I desire you, but I've committed to *her*."

"She took you from me. Where is she now?"

"With her aunt. She's staying out of everyone's sight," he said indifferently.

"You don't care about her!" Eustacia said triumphantly. "If you did, you wouldn't speak of her with such indifference."

"I wish that she weren't such a good woman. Then I could be faithful to you without injuring a worthy person."

"You mustn't sacrifice yourself to her out of some sense of duty or honor!" Eustacia said emphatically. "If you don't love her, the kindest thing to do is to leave her. If you do love her, why didn't you go through with the wedding?"

"The license wasn't right, and Tamsin ran away before I could get another."

"I'm nothing to you, then!"

"That isn't true. Will you go to America with me? I have relatives in Wisconsin."

"I have to think about it. America is so far away."

The two left the barrow, and Diggory couldn't hear any more. He returned to his wagon and considered what he had heard. "My poor Tamsie," he thought.

CHAPTER 4

Early the next morning, Diggory headed to the Vye house, which few ever visited. Apart from the Yeobrights, the Vyes were the area's only genteel people. When Diggory entered the garden, Captain Vye recognized him as his traveling companion but said only, "Ah, ruddleman. You here? Would you like a glass of rum?"

"No thank you. My business is with Miss Vye."

The captain looked him over from cap to shoes. "Come inside."

Cap in hands, Diggory waited for Eustacia on the kitchen's window bench. "The young lady isn't up yet?" he asked the maid.

"Not quite yet."

"Then, I'll step outside. If she's willing to see me, please send me word and I'll come in." Diggory left the house and waited outside. A considerable time elapsed. Then Eustacia came leisurely toward him.

"May I speak with you?" Diggory asked.

"Yes."

"I've made bold, Miss, to come tell you some strange news that I've heard about Mr. Wildeve. He's caused trouble in a household. I believe you might have the power to end the trouble."

"What is it?"

"He may refuse to marry Tamsin Yeobright."

Eustacia replied coldly, "I don't wish to listen to this, and I certainly won't interfere."

"You're the only lady on the heath, and I think you might be able to influence Mr. Wildeve. He'd marry Tamsin right away if there weren't another woman involved. I think that he occasionally meets this other woman on the heath. If you were to ask him to treat Tamsin with honor and kindness and give up the other woman, he might do it and save Tamsin much misery."

Eustacia laughed. "You overrate my influence, ruddleman. Besides, Tamsin Yeobright never has been particularly kind to me. Although we live only two miles apart, I've never been invited inside her aunt's house."

"Well, your beauty is sure to give you some power over Mr. Wildeve, Miss."

"Surely I can't persuade him to do what Tamsin herself cannot."

Diggory looked directly at Eustacia. "Miss Vye, I overheard you and Mr. Wildeve at Rainbarrow. You're the woman who stands between Tamsin and Mr. Wildeve."

Eustacia gasped, and her lips trembled. "I have no wish to hear you further. Please leave."

"I must speak, Miss Vye, even if it pains you. Tamsin's situation is worse than yours. For this reason, I ask you to give up Mr. Wildeve."

"I won't," Eustacia said angrily. "I won't be defeated by an inferior woman like her. Her situation is of her own making. She comes between Damon and me and then sends you to plead for her."

"She knows nothing about your relationship with Mr. Wildeve," Diggory said. "I'm the one asking you to give him up."

"I wouldn't have cared for him if there had been a better man near."

Diggory looked hopeful. "Here's what I propose. As a ruddleman, I travel a lot, including near Budmouth. It's a wonderful place, with bands playing, ladies and gentlemen walking up and down, and a shining sea bending into the land like a bow."

"I know Budmouth better than you," Eustacia said disdainfully. "I was born there. I wish I were there now."

"If you were, in a week you'd think no more of Mr. Wildeve than of some peasant. I can get you to Budmouth."

"How?" Eustacia asked with intense curiosity.

"My uncle knows a rich widow who has a beautiful house facing the sea. This lady is old and lame. She'd like a companion to read and sing to her. She has advertised in the newspapers and has tried half a dozen women, but she hasn't found anyone who pleases her. She'd jump to get you, and my uncle would arrange it all."

"I'd have to work?"

"Not really. All you'd have to do is easy things like read to her. You wouldn't be wanted until New Year's Day. Think of the life you'd lead, the company you'd keep, and the kind of gentleman you'd marry."

"I'd be little more than a servant!" she said indignantly. "Please go."

Feeling hopeless, Diggory left. He saw Elizabeth Yeobright walking toward the inn and went up to her. "May I have a word with you, Mrs. Yeobright?"

"Certainly."

"Mr. Wildeve isn't the only man who has asked Tamsin to marry him. I asked her two years ago. I'd be glad to marry her."

Elizabeth looked him over.

"Looks aren't everything," Diggory said. "I've saved money. If you dislike my redness, I can earn my living another way."

"I thank you for your interest in my niece, but she's devoted to Mr. Wildeve. What was her answer when you proposed to her?"

"She wrote that you'd object to me and that she didn't love me the way a woman loves a man she wants to marry."

"You've been good to her, and I'm grateful.

But since she was unwilling to be your wife, that settles the matter as far as I'm concerned."

"But there's a difference between then and now, ma'am. She's in distress now. If you were to think favorably of me and talk to her about me, she might change her mind."

Elizabeth shook her head. "Tamsin and I both think that she should marry Mr. Wildeve if she's to save her reputation. If they marry soon, everyone will believe that an accident initially prevented the wedding. If not, the situation will hurt her reputation. Now, please excuse me. I must walk on."

When Elizabeth reached the inn, Damon was in. He showed her silently into the parlor and closed the door.

Elizabeth began, "I want you to know that another man has proposed to Tamsin."

"Who?" Damon asked with surprise.

"The ruddleman, Diggory Venn. He's been in love with her longer than she's been in love with you. He proposed to her two years ago. At that time she refused him. He's seen her lately, and he's asked me for permission to pay his addresses to her. She might not refuse him a second time. Tamsin likes him and respects his constancy. She's much annoyed at her present awkward situation."

"She never told me about another man. Well, if she wants him, she should have him."

"Before I encourage him, I must have your word that you won't interfere."

"I wouldn't interfere, but they aren't engaged yet. How do you know that Tamsin would accept him?"

"I believe that she'll accept him in time. I have influence over her and will strongly recommend him."

"And strongly speak *against* me."

"I certainly won't praise you," she said dryly. "I want you to tell her that she no longer should think of you as a possible husband."

"I can't do that, Mrs. Yeobright."

"So, you *do* interfere!"

"I need some time to think about this. May I let you know in a day or two?"

"Yes," she said, "provided that you promise not to communicate with Tamsin without my knowledge."

"I promise," he said.

That evening Damon went to Eustacia's house. By throwing a stone at the shutter of her bedroom window, he attracted her attention without attracting her grandfather's.

From inside, she said, "I hear you. Wait for me."

After about twenty minutes, she appeared.

"You wouldn't keep me waiting so long if you knew what I've come about," Damon said bitterly.

"What's happened?" Eustacia asked.

"Matters have come to a head. Mrs. Yeobright wants me to give up Tamsin because another man, the ruddleman Diggory Venn, is anxious to marry her."

"So, now you want me because you can't have *her*." Suddenly Eustacia felt less desire for Damon. If Tamsin didn't want him, why should *she*? She became more aware of her social superiority to him.

"Will you go to America with me?" Damon asked.

"If it could be London, or even Budmouth, instead of America," she murmured. "This is too serious a matter for me to decide immediately."

"Last month you loved me enough to go anywhere with me."

"And you loved Tamsin."

"If you don't agree to go with me, and agree soon, I'll go by myself."

"Or try Tamsin again."

"Come to Bristol with me, marry me, and go to America with me."

"I need to think about it."

"I'll come to Rainbarrow a week from Monday. Meet me there, and let me know."

"Very well."

Eustacia watched his shadowy form until it disappeared. She now thought of him as mediocre. She went inside. Her grandfather had just returned from the inn.

"Have you heard the news, Eustacia? Clym Yeobright is coming home next week to spend Christmas with his mother. You've never met him. He's a fine fellow now."

"Where has he been living all these years?"

"In Paris."

A few days before Christmas, the Yeobright household was busy preparing for Clym's arrival. While picking out apples, Tamsin said to her aunt, "Why don't people judge me by my acts? I wish all supposedly good women were as good as I am."

"Strangers don't see you as I do," Elizabeth said. "They judge from false report."

Tamsin's lips quivered, and tears came into her eyes.

"Tamsin, do you still want to marry Damon?" her aunt asked.

"Yes, and I *will* marry him."

"Well, first he has to repeat his offer."

"Are you going to tell Clym about my would-be marriage? Please don't. He loved me once, and my troubles would pain him. I'll tell him myself in a week or two."

"Very well," her aunt replied.

CHAPTER 5

Eustacia was in her kitchen when she overheard her grandfather speaking with Humphrey and Sam.

"Clym Yeobright never should have left home," Captain Vye said. "He should have been a farmer, like his father."

"He's been in Paris. He's the manager of a diamond company," Humphrey said.

When Captain Vye was out of hearing, Humphrey said to Sam, "Eustacia Vye and Clym Yeobright would make a pretty pair, huh? Both like niceties. Both have book knowledge. They seem made for each other. Clym's family is as good as hers. His father was only a farmer, but his mother's a lady. They say that Clym can talk French."

"That's bad trouble about his cousin Tamsin," Sam said. "Clym won't be happy to learn of it."

"Poor maid. Her heart's been aching. Her health is suffering, I hear. She always stays indoors."

Eustacia had listened intently. A young, clever man was coming from Paris. She started daydreaming about Clement Yeobright.

At twilight Eustacia put on her bonnet and walked in the direction of Blooms End. At the same time, Tamsin and her aunt headed toward the highway to meet Clym.

When Eustacia reached Blooms End, she found it dark and silent. Clearly, Clym hadn't come yet. Eustacia turned back for home. She soon came upon Tamsin, Elizabeth, and Clym. As she passed, Clym greeted her: "Good evening."

She murmured a reply and strained her eyes to glimpse him, but it was too dark. All the way home, she thought of him, remembering the sound of his voice. She found her grandfather sitting by the fire.

Coming forward and stretching her soft hands over the warmth, she asked, "Why aren't we ever friendly with the Yeobrights? They seem to be nice people."

"I don't know," the captain replied. "I liked Michael Yeobright, Clym's father, but I think you'd find the Yeobrights too countrified."

"Mrs. Yeobright is ladylike, isn't she? Isn't she the daughter of a clergyman?"

"Yes."

That night Eustacia dreamed that she was dancing to wonderful music, with a man in silver armor. From under his radiant helmet, he whispered into her ear. He started to remove his helmet to kiss her, but the dream ended. She woke up, thinking, "If only I'd seen his face!" Without even having seen him, she was half in love with Clym Yeobright.

Two days before Christmas, at dusk, a group of men and boys came to the Vye house. Captain Vye had given them permission to use the house as a place to rehearse a Christmas play. Eustacia learned that they would be performing the play at the Yeobrights' Christmas party. In order to go and observe Clym, she decided to take the place of one of the actors, sixteen-year-old Charlie.

When Charlie was about to leave, Eustacia pointed to a seat by the fire and said, "Charlie, come here."

Blushing, Charlie did as asked.

"Which part do you play?" she asked.

"A knight," he replied.

"Is it a long part?"

"About nine lines."

"Can you recite them to me?"

"If you'd like to hear them." He recited the lines.

Eustacia had heard them before. As soon as Charlie finished, she repeated them.

Wide-eyed with admiration, Charlie said, "Well, you're a clever lady!"

"I've heard it before," Eustacia said quietly. "Would you do anything to please me, Charlie?"

"I'd do a lot, Miss."

"Would you let me play your part for one night?"

"How could you? They'd all see that you're a woman."

"I'll be dressed in armor. Will you lend me your costume, let me take your place for an hour or two on Christmas night, and swear to keep this a secret? You can say that a cousin of Miss Vye is taking your place. What must I give you for you to agree to this? Half a crown?"

Charlie shook his head.

"Five shillings?"

He shook his head again. "I don't want money. Just let me hold your hand for half an hour."

Eustacia considered. "Make it fifteen minutes."

"OK."

"Very well. I'll allow you to hold my hand as soon as you bring the costume. That's all for now."

Charlie left.

Eustacia was excited. Even if her trick was exposed, people simply would think it a clever joke.

The next evening, Charlie brought Eustacia the costume. "Here are the things," he said. "And now . . ."

"The payment," she said. "I'm ready."

Charlie tenderly took one of her hands in both

of his and caressed it for about fifteen minutes.

Then Eustacia withdrew her hand and said coldly, "That completes our agreement."

The next evening, Eustacia made her way to Blooms End dressed as a knight. The sounds of music and dancing came from inside. The performers were gathering outside. When the dancing ceased, they entered.

After the knight played by Eustacia was slain, she was able to look around while playing dead. She noticed that Tamsin wasn't present. Then she spotted the person she was looking for: Clym. He had a handsome, intelligent face.

The play ended, and Timothy Fairway entered. Clym went forward to welcome him.

Timothy said to everyone present, "I never would have recognized this gentleman if I'd seen him anywhere else. He's so changed."

The performers were preparing to leave, but Elizabeth asked them to sit down and have supper. Eustacia was happy at the chance to stay longer.

Elizabeth murmured a few words to Clym, who brought the performers beef, bread, cake, and wine. He and his mother served the performers, so that their maid could sit as a guest. Except for Eustacia, the performers took off their helmets and began to eat and drink.

"Won't you have some?" Clym asked Eustacia as he stood before her, tray in hand.

"No thank you," she replied.

Clym eyed her closely. "Try a glass of mead or wine."

Because she could drink beneath her disguise, Eustacia accepted some wine, and Clym moved on. Eustacia saw him open a door. There stood Tamsin, anxious and pale. Apparently glad to see her, Clym pressed her hand and said, "Tamsie, I'm glad that you've decided to come down."

"No," she said quickly. "I came only to speak to you."

"Why don't you join us?"

"I'd rather not. You and I will have plenty of time together now that you're going to stay for a good, long holiday. It isn't half as pleasant without you."

"Are you unwell?"

"A little."

Clym followed Tamsin into a room and closed the door behind them.

The heat flew into Eustacia's cheeks. She instantly guessed that Clym didn't know about Tamsin's situation with regard to Damon. Suddenly Eustacia felt wildly jealous of Tamsin. There was no knowing what affection Clym and Tamsin might develop for each other.

Clym returned without Tamsin. Once again, he looked closely at Eustacia. Uncomfortable in her male role, she slipped outside.

While she was looking at the moon, Clym quietly came outside and approached her. "I'd like to ask you an odd question. Are you a woman?"

"Yes."

His eyes lingered on her with great interest. "Do women often perform in the Christmas play now? They never used to."

"They don't now either."

"Why did *you*?"

"To find excitement and shake off depression," she said in low tones.

"What has depressed you?"

"Life."

After a long silence, Clym asked, "Did you find excitement?"

"Now, perhaps."

"I would have asked you to our party if I'd known that you wanted to come. Have I ever met you before?"

"No."

"Won't you come back in and stay as long as you like?"

"No. I don't want anyone to recognize me."

"I won't intrude on you any longer. Good night." Clym went to the back of the house, where he walked up and down for some time before reentering.

Warmed by an inner fire, Eustacia headed home. She felt some misery at the thought that it was Tamsin, not she, who would be spending the coming days with Clym. Suddenly she remembered that she had promised to meet Damon at

Rainbarrow at eight o' clock. He probably had come, waited in the cold, and left. "Serves him right," she thought. Now she wished that he *had* married Tamsin.

CHAPTER 6

The next day, during one of her walks, Eustacia came across Diggory. She thought, "He's handsome, intelligent, and well off, but it isn't likely that Tamsin will accept him."

Taking off his cap, Diggory said, "Good morning, Miss," with no ill will.

"Good morning, ruddleman," Eustacia said without lifting her eyes to his. The roof and chimney of Diggory's wagon showed behind some vegetation. "Are you remaining in this area?" she asked with more interest.

"Yes."

"Because of Miss Yeobright?" Her face seemed to ask for a truce.

"Yes, Miss, because of her."

Eustacia was about to pass by when she noticed Damon approaching. He hadn't seen her. "Will you allow me to rest a few minutes inside your wagon?" she asked Diggory.

"Certainly, Miss."

Eustacia followed Diggory to the wagon. He

placed a three-legged stool inside. "That's the best I can do for you," he said, stepping back out.

Eustacia bounded inside. She soon heard Diggory and Damon greet each other with a cool "Good day." And Damon passed on.

Eustacia got out of the wagon, and Diggory said, "That was Mr. Wildeve who passed, Miss."

To Diggory's surprise, Eustacia said, "Yes. I saw him coming."

"Now I understand why Mr. Wildeve waited at Rainbarrow a long time yesterday, for a woman who never came," Diggory said.

"I wish I knew what to do," Eustacia said with uncharacteristic openness. "I don't want to be uncivil to him, but I don't want to see him again, and there are some items that I'd like to return to him."

"If you like, I'll bring them to him, along with a note telling him that you don't want to see him anymore. That would be the most straight-forward way of letting him know your mind."

"I'll do that," Eustacia said. "Come to my house, and I'll bring the items out to you."

When they reached the house, Eustacia went inside and soon came back out with a package and a note. Placing them in Diggory's hands, she said, "Why are you so ready to take these for me? Are you still anxious to promote Tamsin's marriage to Mr. Wildeve?"

"I'd rather have married her myself," he said

quietly. "But if she can't be happy without Mr. Wildeve, I'll help her get him."

Eustacia looked at him with curiosity, thinking, "What a strange sort of love!" Part of her respected Diggory for his selflessness; the other part thought him ridiculous. "Then, we both want the same thing," she said.

"Why have you changed your mind?" Diggory asked.

"I can't tell you that," Eustacia said coldly.

Diggory pocketed the letter, bowed to Eustacia, and left.

That night, when Damon came to Rainbarrow, it was Diggory who met him. "These are for you," Diggory said.

Startled, Damon took the package and note. "I don't understand."

"Read the note, and you will." Diggory lit a candle that he had brought and held it over the note.

Damon opened the note and read:

Mr. Wildeve,

    I've decided that we must end our acquaintance. The bearer of this note is returning the small items that you gave me early in our friendship.

                    Eustacia Vye

Annoyed, Damon said, "She's made a fool of me. Well, I suppose I deserve it, considering how I've played with both women. But why have you served as the messenger, against your own interests? Mrs. Yeobright says that you're going to marry Tamsin."

"What? When did she say so? I'll go straight to her." Diggory hurried away.

Humiliated, Damon thought, "The only thing I can do now is marry Tamsin. Then Eustacia will regret the way she's treated me."

Back at his wagon, Diggory groomed and put on a suit with no red in it. Then he set off toward Blooms End. When he arrived at the gate, he saw Tamsin and Damon on the porch. Tamsin went inside, and Damon came toward the gate.

"You've been quick about it," Diggory said bitterly.

"And you've been too slow. I've claimed her and got her. Good night, ruddleman!" And Damon walked away.

Diggory's heart sank, and he returned to his wagon.

"That was Damon," Tamsin told her aunt. "He wants the wedding to take place the day after tomorrow, privately, at his parish's church."

"Indeed! And what did you say?"

"I've agreed," Tamsin said firmly. "I'm a practical woman now. I'd marry him under any circumstances since . . . since Clym's letter."

A letter was lying on Elizabeth's sewing basket. It was from Clym, who was visiting friends. Elizabeth reopened it and read it for the tenth time that day:

> I've heard scandalous gossip about Tamsin and Mr. Wildeve. I keep denying the rumors, but I wonder how they originated. It's ridiculous that a woman like Tamsin would be jilted on her wedding day. What has happened?

"Yes," Elizabeth said sadly, putting the letter down. "If you think you can marry him, do so. My power over your welfare came to an end when you went to Anglebury with him." She continued with some bitterness, "In fact, why consult me now?" Then she softened. She rose, kissed Tamsin, and asked, "Do you want me to give you away?"

"No, I won't ask you to come," Tamsin said sadly. "It would be unpleasant. Let there be only strangers there, none of my relatives. I'd prefer that."

CHAPTER 7

The morning of the wedding, Tamsin arranged her hair into seven braids. She put on a dress of blue silk and, at nine o'clock, hurried out.

"I'll call on you this afternoon and bring the cake," Elizabeth said with forced cheerfulness. "If Clym has returned by then, maybe he'll come too. I want to show Mr. Wildeve that I bear him no ill will. God bless you!"

Seeing her aunt's worn, tear-streaked face, Tamsin ran back. Her aunt came forward, and the two women embraced. Elizabeth sobbed, "Oh, Tamsie!"

"Goodbye!" Tamsin cried, and left.

About a half hour later, Clym returned to Blooms End. "What's this I've heard about Tamsin and Mr. Wildeve?" he asked his mother.

"Some of it is true," Elizabeth said quietly, "but it's all right now, I hope." She looked at the clock.

"True?"

"Tamsin has gone to him."

"Is this what has made Tamsin sad and ill?"

"Yes. You must listen and not be angry. What we've done is for the best." She then told Clym what had happened.

Clym was greatly surprised and troubled. "You were wrong not to share this with me."

"I thought it might disturb you so much that you'd quit your job or otherwise ruin your career prospects, so I didn't say anything."

"Tamsin being married while we're sitting here! Well, I suppose there was nothing else to do." Clym thought for a while. "I don't think it's kind to Tamsin to let her be married like this, with neither of us there to keep up her spirits and show that we care about her. She hasn't disgraced herself or done anything to deserve that. It's bad enough that the wedding should be so hurried and unceremonious, without our keeping away from it in addition. I'm going."

"It's over by now," his mother said with a sigh.

"Then, I'll be there to see them come out of the church. I don't like your keeping me in ignorance, Mother." He took up his hat and hastily left the house.

Elizabeth sat deep in unhappy thought.

A few minutes later Clym returned, accompanied by Diggory. "I'm too late," Clym said.

"Is she married?" Elizabeth asked Diggory.

"Yes, ma'am. I came to tell you," he said in a voice husky with emotion.

"Who gave her away?"

"Miss Vye."

"What?"

"Who's Miss Vye?" Clym asked.

"Captain Vye's granddaughter," Diggory said.

"A proud girl from Budmouth," Elizabeth said. "I don't like her."

"How did Miss Vye come to have anything to do with it?"

"She was walking that way," Diggory lied, "and there wasn't anyone else to act as a witness." Actually, Diggory had brought Eustacia. "She signed the book as a witness, and Tamsin thanked her for her kindness. Now I'll wish you good morning," Diggory said sadly. He put on his cap, went out, and prepared to leave Egdon.

CHAPTER 8

While Timothy Fairway was cutting men's hair, as he did every Sunday, the group noticed Clym walking on the heath.

"Why do you think he's still in Egdon?" Timothy asked. "A man who's doing well elsewhere doesn't stay two or three weeks for nothing."

Clym noticed the group and came over. After looking at their faces, he said, "Now, let me guess what you've been talking about: me."

"You're right, Mr. Yeobright," Timothy admitted. "We were wondering why you've been staying here so long."

"I'll tell you," Clym said. "I've come home because I can be most useful here. I've realized that the diamond business is vain and completely unimportant. I've decided to give it up and follow some occupation among the people I know best. I've come home to carry out my plan. I'll run a day school near Egdon and a night school in Blooms End. But I must study first, to become qualified. Now, neighbors, I must go." Clym resumed his walk across the heath.

"He won't do it," Timothy said. "In a few weeks, he'll change his mind."

"It's good of him," Humphrey said, "but I think he'd better stick with the diamond business."

When he arrived home, Clym told his mother, "I'm not going back to Paris. I've given up the diamond business."

Elizabeth looked at him in pained surprise.

"I'm going to take an entirely new direction."

"I'm astonished, Clym. How can you want to do better than you've been doing?"

"I don't want to do better in the way that you mean. I suppose I'll be doing worse. I hate the diamond business. I want to do something worthwhile before I die. I want to teach those who are poor and ignorant. I want to be a schoolmaster."

"After all the progress you've made in the diamond trade? What a waste!"

"I can't waste my time in the diamond trade" he said. "The people here need educating, and I want to help them."

That afternoon, Clym and his mother walked on the heath. When the inn was visible, Clym said, "Are you going to call on Tamsin?"

"Yes."

"In that case, I'll branch off here, Mother.

I've been hearing about Miss Vye. Apparently, she's quite educated. I'd like to ask her if she'll teach in my school."

Elizabeth didn't like hearing this. When they parted, she watched Clym with worry in her face. She abandoned the idea of visiting Tamsin and turned back.

At the Vye house, Clym greeted Eustacia warmly and asked if she would like to teach in his planned school. "The people around here would greatly benefit."

"I don't want to," she said flatly. "I don't particularly like these people. Sometimes I hate them."

Disappointed, Clym asked, "You dislike it here?"

"I hate the heath, except when the heather blooms."

"I love the heath. I find it exhilarating, strengthening, and soothing. I'd rather live here than anywhere else in the world."

"You, who have lived in Paris!"

"I remember when I had your longing for city life. Five years in a big city would cure you of that."

"Heaven send me such a cure!"

During his walk home, Clym thought about Eustacia—primarily about her beauty. At home, he went up to the room that would be his study and started unpacking his books and arranging them on shelves. The next day, he read all day.

Then he decided to walk on the heath. When he returned home an hour and a half later, his mother asked, "Where have you been, Clym?"

"On the heath."

"You'll meet Eustacia Vye if you go up there."

"Yes, I met her this evening," Clym said reluctantly.

"I wondered if you had."

"It wasn't arranged."

"I don't know why you're interested in Eustacia Vye."

Throughout the coming weeks, Clym studied at home and walked much, always in the direction of the Vye residence.

"Lately, I've spent much time with Eustacia Vye," he told his mother one night.

"It troubles me, Clym. You're wasting your life here, and it's because of her. This teaching idea is because of her."

Clym looked hard at his mother. "You know that isn't true. You're mistaken about Eustacia."

"How am I mistaken? She's lazy, dissatisfied, and haughty. I don't consider her a particularly good woman. Why connect yourself with her?"

"If I start a school, an educated woman will be a great help to me."

"Do you intend to marry her?"

"It would be premature to say that. But consider the advantages of my doing so. She . . ."

"She has no money."

"She's well-educated. She'd make a good schoolmistress. I no longer intend to teach the poorest and most ignorant. I can do better than that. I can establish a good private school for farmers' sons. With the assistance of a wife like Eustacia, I should end up as the head of one of the best schools in the county."

"Oh, Clym! You're blinded. It was a bad day when you first set eyes on Eustacia Vye. And your plan is merely an attempt to justify the folly that has seized you."

"That's not true," he said firmly.

"I'm trying to save you from sorrow. That woman's a hussy!"

Clym reddened. He placed his hand on his mother's shoulder and said, "Don't say any more, or I'll be led to answer you in a way that we'll both regret."

The next day was gloomy at Blooms End. Clym stayed in his study, in front of open books, but he had trouble concentrating. That evening he went to Rainbarrow. Eustacia came to meet him there. Cloaked, she appeared with an upturned face at the base of the barrow. Clym descended. In a moment the two were embracing and kissing.

"My Eustacia!"

"Clym, dearest! Has it seemed long since you last saw me?"

"It has seemed sad. I love you beyond all description. Let me look at your moonlit face and dwell on every line and curve."

"We won't always love like this. It will vanish. I loved another man once, and now I love you."

"Don't talk like that, Eustacia!"

"Your mother will find out that you meet me, and she'll influence you against me."

"She already knows."

"Does she speak against me?"

Clym intentionally ignored the question. "I want you to be my wife. Will you marry me?"

"I need to think about it. Tell me about Paris."

"Will you be mine?"

"I won't be anyone else's. Does that satisfy you?"

"For now."

"Will you be going back to Paris?"

"No."

"If you'll agree to go back, I'll marry you."

"I'm not going back, Eustacia."

"You should be doing better things than this education plan of yours."

"You're ambitious for luxury, Eustacia, whereas I would gladly live and die here if I had good work to do."

"Don't mistake me, Clym," Eustacia said. "I'd like to be in Paris, but I love you for yourself. To be your wife and live in Paris would be heaven, but I'd rather live with you in a shack than not be yours." Eustacia paused. "How terrible it would be if I ever stopped loving you."

"Don't say such things. It's too late for me to speak to your grandfather tonight. Tomorrow I'll ask his permission to marry you. Do you think that he'll object?"

"I'll speak to him. I'm so used to being my own mistress that it didn't even occur to me that we should ask his permission."

After they parted, Clym walked home feeling troubled. He sensed that he and Eustacia didn't value the same things. How would his becoming a teacher be conducive to Eustacia's happiness? And how would his marriage not make his mother unhappy?

CHAPTER 9

The next time that Clym saw Eustacia, she said that her grandfather had given permission for them to marry.

A few days later, after a morning visit to Tamsin, Elizabeth said to Clym, "I've heard an incredible thing. Captain Vye has said, at the inn, that you and his daughter are engaged."

"We are," Clym said.

"You'll take her to Paris?"

"I'm not going back to Paris."

"What will you do with her, then?"

"Run a school in Budmouth."

"How can you? The place already is overrun with schoolmasters. You have no special qualifications. The situation would be bad even if Eustacia Vye were a good woman."

"She *is* a good woman."

"No lady would roam around the heath day and night as she does. And that's not all. There used to be something between Damon and her. I'm sure of it."

"Eustacia has told me that she once loved another man."

"She won't be a good wife. I wish I hadn't lived to see this." Elizabeth turned to the window. Her breath came quickly, and her lips trembled. "By choosing such a sensuous, idle woman you show that you don't know what's best. She's unworthy!"

Controlling his anger, Clym said, "I'm going to meet with Eustacia now. I told her that you'd come with me. Will you come?"

"Certainly not!"

"Very well," Clym said angrily, and he left.

When Clym showed up alone, Eustacia said, "Oh. Your mother refused to come. You look upset."

"Let's walk," Clym said. Hand in hand, they walked along the valley.

"I wish I was sure of never losing you," she said.

Taking her in his arms, Clym said, "You can be sure of me, darling. We'll be married at once."

"Oh, Clym!"

"Do you agree? I've saved money. If you'll agree, we'll live in a small cottage somewhere on the heath until I can buy a house in Budmouth for the school."

"How long will we have to live in the cottage?"

"About six months, until I've finished my studying."

"Dearest, let's set the date."

They decided on two weeks later.

That evening, Clym packed his belongings. The next morning he walked about four miles to an empty cottage, surrounded by fir trees, that he previously had noticed. Then he journeyed about a mile farther to the village in which the cottage's owner lived. Returning with him, Clym arranged to rent the cottage, which was in Alderworth.

Clym returned to Blooms End through a drizzle that left him damp and weary. That evening and the following morning, he concluded arrangements for his departure. The next step was to get some furniture. He would do this in Anglebury, some miles beyond his new residence.

Before leaving, Clym approached his mother where she sat by the window. "Mother, I'm leaving," he said, holding out his hand. "Do we part as friends?"

"Of course, Clym."

"Eustacia and I are going to be married on the twenty-fifth. After that, you must come and see us at Alderworth."

"I don't think so."

"That won't be my fault or Eustacia's, then. Goodbye." He kissed his mother's cheek and left in misery.

After Clym left, his mother wept. The rest of the day she did nothing but walk up and down the garden path. That night, she slept little.

The next day, Tamsin visited her aunt.

"You look content, Tamsie," Elizabeth said. "How's Damon?"

"He's well."

"Is he kind to you?"

"Overall." Tamsin blushed and hesitated. "He doesn't give me any money, and I need some to buy little things for myself. Should I ask him for some money?"

"Of course you should."

"I've heard about Clym and Eustacia Vye. I know you're upset. That's why I've come."

Elizabeth started to weep. "Oh, Tamsin, do you think that he hates me?"

"Of course not. He just loves Miss Vye."

"It breaks my heart that he's chosen unwisely."

"There are worse women than Eustacia Vye."

"And many better. I'm sure that she's the one who led Damon to act as he did."

"No," Tamsin said eagerly. "Damon thought of her only before he knew me. It was nothing but a flirtation."

"Well, there's no point in discussing that now."

"Don't fret, Aunt. I'll come to see you every day."

For one week, Tamsin did visit her aunt every day. She told Elizabeth about Clym's wedding preparations. The next week, however, she was unwell and didn't visit.

Damon learned of the upcoming marriage from a visitor to his inn. "Eustacia Vye is marrying Clym Yeobright?"

"Yes," the visitor said. "He's been creeping around with her all spring. Miss Vye's maid says that Miss Vye is crazy about him."

Damon felt heartache. The old longing for Eustacia returned, mainly because he was jealous.

The morning of the wedding, Elizabeth declined to attend the ceremony. She sat looking out at the valley, alive with butterflies and noisy grasshoppers. She imagined the scene at the church. At noon she heard East Egdon's church bells announcing her son's marriage. "It's over," she muttered.

Toward evening Damon came. Since his marriage, he'd behaved very courteously toward Elizabeth, and she had shown him a cool cordiality. "Tamsin isn't able to come," Damon told her. "She's at the wedding celebration. Captain Vye sent a carriage for her."

"Why didn't you go with Tamsin?"

"I couldn't," Damon said, reddening slightly. "It was a busy morning at the inn. In fact, I'd better get back." And he left.

Elizabeth's husband had set aside some money for Tamsin and Clym. Because Tamsin needed money and Clym had just gotten married, Elizabeth decided that this would be a good time to give Tamsin and Clym the money. She went upstairs and took a small box from a locked drawer. She poured out a hundred guineas, divided the coins into two equal piles, and tied up each pile of fifty in a small canvas bag. Then she went down to the garden, gave her handyman Christian Cantle the bags, told him what they contained, and asked him to go to the Vye residence and give one bag to Tamsin and the other to Clym. Christian promised to do that and set out.

On the way, however, friends persuaded Christian to stop off at the inn. After a while, Christian said, "Well, I'd better go. I have something to deliver to Mrs. Wildeve."

Overhearing, Damon asked, "What do you have to deliver?"

"It's a secret," Christian answered awkwardly.

"Where are you going?" Damon asked.

"To Captain Vye's. I have to see Mrs. Wildeve."

"I'm going there, too, to fetch her. We can walk together." Damon became lost in thought. Then a look of realization came into his eyes. "Christian has been entrusted with money for Tamsin!" he thought. "Why didn't her aunt give *me* the money when I saw her this morning? She doesn't trust me!" Insulted, Damon determined to get revenge. He grabbed a pair of dice and left with Christian.

Unnoticed, Diggory had been sitting in the inn's chimney-corner. He now rose and wished everyone good night.

Damon and Christian plunged into the heath. It was a stagnant, warm, misty night.

"Are you carrying money to Mrs. Wildeve?" Damon asked Christian.

Christian didn't answer.

"Why don't you just give it to me? I'm her husband. What belongs to her belongs to me."

"I was instructed to give it directly to Mrs. Wildeve," Christian said.

When they were almost to Rainbarrow, Damon said, "It's very warm. Let's sit down and rest for a few minutes." Damon flung himself down on the soft ferns, and Christian sat nearby. After some time, Damon took out the dice and convinced Christian to bet for money. At first, Christian bet with his own money, and lost. Then he started betting with the money that Elizabeth had entrusted to his care. Eventually, Christian lost all of it to Damon.

Flinging himself down in remorse, Christian cried, "What will I do?"

"Live on," Damon said coldly.

"Half of that money is Mr. Clym's," Christian said softly. "I was supposed to give him fifty guineas."

"Oh? Well, it would have been more gracious of Mrs. Yeobright to give them to the bride, Eustacia. But they're in *my* hands now."

In confusion and despair, Christian hurried away.

Damon was about to head back to the inn when Diggory emerged from behind a bush. Damon stared. Diggory looked at him coldly and sat down where Christian had been seated. "Now *I'll* place bets," Diggory said.

"You were watching us from behind that bush?" Damon asked.

"Yes. Put your bet down. Or don't you have the guts?"

The two men started to bet. Eventually Diggory won all hundred of the guineas.

Furious, Damon stormed back to the inn.

Diggory headed toward the high road and waited. In about half an hour, a carriage approached. Tamsin was inside. Diggory hailed the driver, who halted the carriage. "Excuse me for stopping you, Mrs. Wildeve," Diggory said to Tamsin. "I have something to give you from Mrs. Yeobright." Having failed to hear Christian say that half of the guineas were intended for Clym, Diggory handed Tamsin all one hundred. Surprised, Tamsin took the bags. "That's all, ma'am," Diggory said. "Good night." And he left.

CHAPTER 10

The July sun shone over Egdon and fired its purple heather to scarlet. Clym and Eustacia were living in happy monotony at the cottage in Alderworth. When it rained, they were happy because they could stay indoors together. When the weather was fine, they were happy because they could sit together on the hills.

After several honeymoon-like weeks, Clym returned to his studies. Eustacia had hoped that, once married to Clym, she would convince him to return to Paris. His books indicated otherwise.

The day after the wedding, Tamsin had sent her aunt a note of thanks for the generous gift, without specifying the sum. She had been surprised by the large amount of money. Needing money of her own, she said nothing about the money to Damon, and Damon, ashamed of his underhanded attempt to take the money, said nothing to Tamsin. Out of fear and shame, Christian too concealed the betting incident.

Elizabeth began to wonder why Clym never

had sent her a thank-you note for the fifty guineas. It wasn't like him to bear such resentment that he wouldn't even thank her for a generous gift. Elizabeth then heard that Eustacia was coming to visit her grandfather. She determined to walk to Captain Vye's house and ask Eustacia if Clym had received the money.

When Christian learned where Elizabeth was going, he finally told her about his losing the money to Damon.

"What? Is he going to keep the money?" Elizabeth cried.

"I hope not!" Christian said with great distress. "He said that you should have given Mr. Clym's share to Eustacia. Maybe he'll do that himself, or already did."

The more that Elizabeth thought about this, the more likely it seemed. Filled with anger, she hurried off to Eustacia. Had her daughter-in-law taken the fifty guineas and not told Clym? Elizabeth's resentment toward Eustacia greatly increased. When she reached Captain Vye's house, she saw Eustacia outside.

As Elizabeth approached, Eustacia observed her coldly.

"I've come to see you," Elizabeth said.

"Indeed!" Eustacia said, still angry and humiliated that Elizabeth had refused to attend the wedding.

"I've come on business only," Elizabeth said more coldly. "Excuse me for asking, but have you received a gift from Mr. Wildeve?"

"A gift?"

"Money."

"What? Never. What do you mean by asking that?" Eustacia demanded passionately. "Why should you think that there's anything between Mr. Wildeve and me? I'm indignant, as any woman would be. You should have a better opinion of me. You've been against me from the start."

"No, I've simply been *for* Clym. I wanted to protect him."

"How dare you imply that Clym needs protection from me! You had no right to speak against me. I've never done you any harm."

"I was firmly convinced that he shouldn't marry you, so I tried to dissuade him."

"I *condescended* to be Clym's wife."

"Condescended?" Elizabeth exclaimed with anger. "My son's family is at least as respectable as yours. It's amusing to hear you speak of condescension."

"It *was* condescension," Eustacia insisted. "And if I'd known then what I know now—that I'd be living on this wild heath a month after my marriage—I would have thought twice before agreeing."

"If there was any deception, it was on your side, not Clym's."

Eustacia's face reddened. "How dare you speak to me like that? If I'd known what my marriage would be like up to this time, I would have refused him. And how dare you suspect me of secretly favoring another man for money!"

"Don't rage at me, madam!" Elizabeth responded. "I'm the one who has lost Clym."

"By your own choice," Eustacia said. "You've caused a division that can't be healed. *I* haven't done anything. Please leave. You're no friend."

"If you show my son half the temper that you've shown me today, you'll find that he can be as hard as steel," Elizabeth said, and she left.

Instead of spending the afternoon with her grandfather, as planned, Eustacia hurried home to Alderworth. She came inside with her face flushed and her eyes moist from crying. She passed by Clym and went upstairs.

Concerned, he followed her. "What's wrong, Eustacia?"

Still wearing her bonnet, she stood looking down at the floor, with her hands clasped in front of her. After a moment, she said, "I've seen your mother. And I'll never see her again!"

"Why?"

"She asked if I had received money from Damon Wildeve!"

"What? There must be some misunderstanding."

"I hate it here! Take me to Paris. Return to the diamond business."

"I've given up that idea. You know that."

"I've continued to hope otherwise."

This disconcerted Clym, but he had no intention of giving up his plan.

After seeing Eustacia, Elizabeth hurried to Tamsin and asked her how many guineas she had received. When Tamsin replied, "A hundred," the mystery was solved.

The next day, Tamsin visited Clym and gave him his half of the money.

"So, that's why my mother asked Eustacia if she had received money," he said. "Tamsin, do you know that they've had a bitter quarrel?"

"Yes," Tamsin said quietly. "Your mother came to my house after seeing Eustacia."

"Was she very upset?"

"Yes."

Clym covered his eyes with his hand.

"Don't worry, Clym. They may still become friends."

He shook his head. "Not two people with such fiery natures."

CHAPTER 11

Clym continued to study. Often he read far into the night. One day, he awoke unable to look at bright light. Eustacia was alarmed. Clym's condition was no better the next morning, so they sent for a doctor.

The doctor arrived toward evening and said that Clym's night studies had strained his eyes. "I don't think you'll be able to read for quite a long time," the doctor said. "For now, stay out of bright light."

A gloom descended on the couple. Eustacia was frightened. What if Clym went blind? What if he couldn't earn a good living? For several weeks, Clym stayed in a darkened room. Eustacia frequently read to him by low lamplight. Then Clym resumed going outside. On his first walk, he came across Humphrey cutting gorse.

"I was sorry to hear about your eyes," Humphrey said. "If you did work like mine, you could continue even with bad eyesight."

"Yes," Clym said indifferently. Then he had a

thought. "Humphrey, how much do you get for cutting gorse?"

"Half a crown for a hundred bundles. I live very well on the wages."

When Clym returned home, Eustacia greeted him from an open window.

"Darling," he said, "I'm much happier. I've discovered a way of earning money while my eyes heal."

"Yes?"

"I'm going to cut gorse."

"No, Clym!" she said with horror.

"We can't go on spending what little money we have. Besides, the outdoor exercise will do me good."

"My grandfather has offered to assist us."

"If I cut gorse, we'll be fairly well off."

"Compared to slaves!" she said bitterly.

The next day, Clym joined Humphrey in cutting gorse. Day after day he rose with the sun and went off to meet Humphrey. He worked from 4 a.m. until noon. Then, when the heat of the day was greatest, he went home and slept an hour or two. Then he went back out and worked until dusk.

After his palms hardened, Clym worked with ease. He was happiest while working. Bees hummed around him. Butterflies quivered in the air and alighted on his bowed back. Grasshoppers leaped over his feet. Bright blue-and-yellow snakes glided past. Baby rabbits sunned themselves on the hills. Sometimes Clym sang or told Humphrey about Parisian life.

One warm afternoon Eustacia walked to Clym. He was chopping gorse. As she approached, she heard him singing. This shocked her. It meant that he didn't rebel against labor that she considered degrading. "I'd rather starve than do this!" she told him. "If I were a man in such a position, I'd curse, not sing! I'll go live with my grandfather again."

"Eustacia! Why do you talk like that? Has your love for me died because I no longer look like a gentleman?"

"I want you to stop this disgraceful laboring. You act against my wishes. We've been married only two months, and you already don't care what I want."

"You're inexperienced, Eustacia. The more I know of life, the more I see that there's nothing especially great in being a gentleman and nothing shameful in being a laborer. Do you begrudge me my cheerfulness?"

"I still feel tenderness for you."

"Your words lack their old flavor. Does your love die when good fortune does?"

"I'm not going to listen to this. I'm going home."

A few days later Eustacia and Clym sat eating dinner. Lately Eustacia's manner had become almost apathetic. Clym, in contrast, was cheerful. "Brighten up, dearest," he said, "We'll be all right.

I'll stop cutting gorse as soon as I can."

"It's so awful for you to be a gorse-cutter—a man who has lived in Paris and who speaks French and German. You're fit for so much better than this. But enough about that. There's going to be a festival in East Egdon this afternoon, and I'm going."

"Should I come fetch you in the evening?"

"If you finish your work early enough. I know the way home, and the heath holds no terrors for me."

He kissed her and went out.

She thought, "Two wasted lives: his and mine. Look what I've come to." She went upstairs and dressed with care. At about five, she left for the festival. She went along the sunny hills at a leisurely pace, following the sound of the East Egdon band. She soon saw the musicians, sitting in a blue wagon, decorated with flowers, with brightly scrubbed red wheels. Dozens of couples were dancing. The young women's curls and braids bounced and flew. Eustacia watched two more dances. Then, being alone, she felt awkward. She decided to walk to a cottage where she might get some refreshment and then return home.

When Eustacia returned to the dance area, it was dusk. She watched the dancing couples with envy. As they spun in the increasing moonlight, she heard someone whisper her name. Turning in surprise, she blushed at the sight of Damon. They hadn't looked each other in the eye since his wedding to Tamsin.

Before she could speak, he said softly, "Do you like dancing as much as ever?"

"Yes," she replied in a low voice.

"Will you dance with me? If you don't want to be recognized, lower your veil."

She did. Damon gave her his arm and took her down on the outside of the ring to the bottom of the dance, which they entered. In two minutes they were involved in the figure and began working their way upward to the top. Eustacia felt a new vitality. She floated round and round on Damon's arm.

Eustacia and Damon danced three dances. Then, tired, Eustacia turned to leave the dance circle. Damon led her to a grassy mound a few yards away. She sat down, and he stood beside her. "The dancing and walking have tired you?" he asked tenderly.

"A little."

"We haven't seen each other in a long time."

"By choice," she said.

"Yes. You broke your promise to meet me at Rainbarrow."

"It's hardly worth speaking of now. We've both formed other ties."

"I'm sorry to hear that your husband is ill."

"He isn't ill; he's just having some trouble with his eyes."

"Yes. I'm sorry for you."

After a pause, Eustacia said, "Have you heard that he's chosen to work as a gorse-cutter?"

"Yes. I hardly believed it."

"It's true. What do you think of me as a gorse-cutter's wife?"

"I think the same as ever of you, Eustacia. Nothing of that sort can degrade you."

"I wish I agreed."

"Is there any chance of Mr. Yeobright regaining his full eyesight?"

"He thinks so, but I don't."

"I was quite surprised to hear that he'd rented a cottage. Like other people, I thought that he'd take you off to a home in Paris. I thought, 'What a gay, bright future she has before her!' He'll return there with you if his sight improves?"

Almost weeping, she didn't answer.

"You don't intend to walk home by yourself?" he asked.

"Yes."

"I'd be glad to keep you company as far as Throop's Corner."

She hesitated.

"Perhaps, after last summer's events, you think it unwise to be seen with me."

"I think no such thing," she said haughtily. "I'll accept whoever's company I choose, whatever Egdon's miserable inhabitants may say."

"Then, let's walk if you're ready."

Eustacia rose and walked beside Damon. Because the heath was so dark, she sometimes stumbled over roots or gorse. At such times, Damon reached out his hand to steady her, holding her until smooth ground returned. For the most part, they walked in silence. They soon saw two men approaching.

"One of those men is Clym," Eustacia said, "He said he'd come to fetch me."

"And the other is Diggory Venn, the ruddleman," Damon said with dislike.

"It's an awkward meeting," she said.

"Neither of them will believe that we met by chance. I should leave you before they recognize me."

"Very well," Eustacia said gloomily.

"Farewell," Damon said tenderly. He plunged across the ferns and gorse, and Eustacia slowly walked on. In several minutes she met Clym and Diggory.

"My journey ends here, Diggory," Clym said. "I turn back with this lady. Good night."

"Good night, Mr. Yeobright," Diggory said. "I hope you'll be better soon." He gave Eustacia a suspicious look. He had detected what Clym, with his poor eyesight, could not: a man withdrawing from Eustacia's side.

As soon as Clym gave Eustacia his arm and led her off the scene, Diggory turned back toward the Quiet Woman Inn, which he reached in half an hour. Diggory ordered a mug of ale and asked the waitress, "Is Mr. Wildeve in?"

Sitting in an inner room, Tamsin heard Diggory's voice. She rarely showed herself when customers were present because she disliked the inn business. However, realizing that there were no other guests, she came out.

"He isn't home yet, Diggory," she said pleasantly. "I expected him sooner than this. He went to East Egdon to buy a horse."

"Did he wear a light-colored jacket?"

"Yes."

"Then, I saw him at Throop's Corner. No doubt, he'll be here soon." He rose and looked for a moment at Tamsin's sweet face, which had acquired a sad look since he last had seen her. "Mr. Wildeve seems to be away a lot."

"Yes. I wish that he'd stay home in the evenings."

Diggory bowed and left.

When Damon returned fifteen minutes later, Tamsin asked, "Where's the horse, Damon?"

"I didn't buy it after all. The price was too high."

CHAPTER 12

The next evening, Damon walked to Clym and Eustacia's cottage and looked in through a window. He saw Eustacia sitting alone. Damon watched her for a minute, then lightly called, "Eustacia!"

She immediately knew that Damon was outside. Clym now entered the room. Eustacia blushed.

"You look flushed, dearest," Clym said.

"I'm warm. I think I'll go outside for a few minutes."

"Shall I go with you?"

"No. I'm only going to the gate." She rose, but before she left the room, there was a loud rapping at the front door.

"I'll go," Eustacia said quickly.

But Clym got to the door before her. He opened it. No one was there. "I wonder what that could have been."

When Damon had softly called to Eustacia, Diggory had come up behind him, knocked at the door, and then vanished around the corner.

"Damn him," Damon thought. "He's been watching me again." Damon withdrew.

When Diggory left the heath, he went to call on Elizabeth, with whom he'd been friendly ever since she had learned his role in getting the guineas to Tamsin. She wondered at the lateness of his visit but made no objection.

Diggory told her what he'd seen.

"Then, there *is* an understanding between Damon and Eustacia!" Elizabeth said.

"Maybe not," Diggory said. "At any rate, I don't believe that any harm has been done yet. It would help if you would visit your son. That might discourage Damon."

"I've wanted to go anyway," Elizabeth said. "I'd be much happier if we were reconciled. I'll go."

While the conversation between Diggory and Elizabeth was taking place, Clym was saying to Eustacia, "I want to heal the breach between my mother and me."

"What do you propose to do?" Eustacia asked with little interest. She was thinking about Damon's attempt to see her.

"I should call on her. Only a fear of irritating her has kept me away. She's getting old, she's lonely, and I'm her only child."

"She has Tamsin."

"Tamsin isn't her daughter. Even if she were,

that wouldn't excuse my staying away. If my mother is willing to be reconciled, will you meet her half way by welcoming her to our house or by accepting a welcome to hers?"

"I won't interfere, but I won't go and visit her."

CHAPTER 13

The last day of August was exceptionally hot. About 11 a.m., Elizabeth started across the heath to Clym and Eustacia's cottage. After walking three miles in the stifling heat, she wished that she had hired someone to drive her at least part of the way. Periodically, she sat down to rest under her parasol. Having never been to the Alderworth cottage, she didn't know its precise location. She tried one ascending path and then another. Retracing her steps, she returned to an open level, where she saw a man working some distance away. She went toward him and asked the way.

The laborer pointed out the direction and added, "Do you see that gorse-cutter going up that footpath, ma'am? That's Clym Yeobright. Just follow him."

Clym walked more rapidly than his mother, but she was able to keep him in sight because he periodically paused to cut gorse. She saw him enter the cottage. When she reached it, Elizabeth felt distressed and unwell. She sat down in the shade of some trees to recover and to consider what she should say to Clym and Eustacia. She sat for twenty minutes or more before she could summon the courage to go to the door. As she rose, she saw a man approaching the gate. He surveyed the cottage, walked around it, and then knocked on the door.

The man was Damon, although Elizabeth didn't know this. When Eustacia opened the door, he asked, "Were you tired the day after the dance?"

"Somewhat," she said.

"Is Clym home?"

"Yes." She opened the door of an adjoining room and asked Damon to come in. Clym was asleep on the hearth rug. His work clothes were beside him.

Damon was startled.

"You won't disturb him," Eustacia said.

"Why is he sleeping?"

"He's been cutting gorse since 4:30 this morning." Eustacia was struck by the contrast between Damon's appearance and Clym's. Damon was elegantly dressed in a new summer suit and hat. "He looked very different when I first met him," she said of Clym. "His hands were as white and soft as mine. Now they're rough and brown."

"Why does he labor that way?" Damon whispered.

"He hates to be idle and wants to earn money, although it isn't much."

"The fates haven't been kind to you, Eustacia."

"I have nothing to thank them for."

"Nor has he, except for their one great gift to him."

"What's that?"

Damon looked her in the eyes. "You."

Eustacia blushed. "I'm a questionable gift," she said. "I thought you meant the gift of contentment—which he has and I don't."

"How can he be content with his situation?"

"He cares about ideas, not appearances."

"Is your marriage a misfortune to you?"

"Not in itself," she said, annoyed. "But the present situation is."

"Sometimes I think it's a judgment on you, Eustacia. You rightly belonged to me."

"Two women couldn't belong to you. You're the one who first turned to someone else."

"I never meant anything by it," Damon said. "It was a passing fancy. My love for you is permanent. That's why it has reasserted itself."

"I thought that Clym was the way to the things that I wanted: music, poetry, passion."

"You married him only for that reason?"

"I married him because I loved him, but I loved him partly because I saw in him a promise of the life that I wanted."

"You've dropped into your old mournful key.

I'm also depressed, because I've lost the thing that matters most to me."

"Damon, you shouldn't talk like that, even if you still love me."

They heard a click at the gate, then a knock at the door. Eustacia went to a window and looked out. She reddened, then paled.

"Should I leave?" Damon asked, standing up.

"I hardly know."

"Who is it?"

"Mrs. Yeobright. I have no idea why she's come. She suspects our past relationship."

"If you'd prefer that she not see me, I'll go into the next room."

Elizabeth knocked more loudly.

Damon and Eustacia heard Clym move in the other room. "Mother," he said.

"He'll go to the door," Eustacia said with relief. "Come this way. I don't want her to see you. She already thinks badly of me."

Eustacia took Damon to the back door. As he stepped outside, she said, "Let this be your last visit, Damon. We've been hot lovers in our time, but it won't do now. Goodbye."

"Goodbye."

Not eager to see her mother-in-law, Eustacia stayed in the garden for a few minutes. Then she returned to the parlor. To her astonishment, Clym was sleeping exactly as before. Apparently, he had murmured "Mother" only in his sleep. He hadn't awakened and answered the door. Eustacia hurried to the door, opened it, and looked out. No one was there.

By now, Elizabeth was following a path hidden from Eustacia's view. She had seen Eustacia look out at her, and she was furious at not having been admitted into the cottage.

Clym awakened and sat up. Eustacia was sitting in a chair nearby, holding a book. "How soundly I slept!" Clym said. "I dreamed that I took you to Blooms End to be reconciled with my mother, but when we got there, we couldn't get in. She kept crying to us for help. What time is it?"

"Two thirty."

"I didn't mean to sleep so long." Clym went to the window and looked out. "Week after week passes, and Mother doesn't come. I thought I'd have heard from her long before this. I must go to see her soon. I think I'd better go alone. I won't go back to the heath today. I'll work in the garden until evening. Then, when it's cooler, I'll walk to Mother's. I wonder if Tamsin has been there lately. Probably not, because she's pregnant."

"I wish you wouldn't go tonight," Eustacia said.

"Why not?"

"Your mother may say something bad about me. If you agree not to go tonight, I promise to go to her house tomorrow, make it up with her, and wait until you fetch me."

"Why do you want to do that now? You've always refused to do that before."

"I can't explain," she answered with an impatient move of her head.

"I don't want to wait another day," he said. "You can go see her afterward."

"Very well."

CHAPTER 14

That evening, Clym set out for Blooms End. On the way, he heard a moan-like sound. Then he saw someone lying near his feet. He stooped and saw his mother's pale face, with closed eyes. His breath left him. He bent lower. She was still alive. Her breath was weak but regular. "Mother!" he cried. "Are you very ill? It's Clym!"

Elizabeth moved her lips and seemed to know him, but she couldn't speak. Clym put his arms around her, lifted her a bit, and said, "Does that hurt you?"

She shook her head.

He lifted her up and moved on at a slow pace. About a mile from Blooms End, Clym spotted a shed. He headed for it. As soon as he arrived, he laid his mother down carefully by the entrance. Then he ran and, with his pocketknife, cut an armful of the driest fern. He spread this within the shed, which was open on one side, and placed his mother on it. Then he ran to Timothy Fairway's house. Timothy rode off to the nearest doctor. On his way, he would stop at the inn and tell Tamsin that her aunt was unwell.

About fifteen minutes later, Clym returned to the shed with Humphrey and others. His mother still was alive.

When Clym had been gone about an hour, Eustacia decided to go toward Blooms End, on the chance of meeting him on his return. As she reached the garden gate, she heard wheels approaching. Her grandfather drove up.

"I can't stay," he said. "I'm driving to East Egdon. I just came to tell you the news. Mr. Wildeve has inherited eleven thousand pounds. His uncle died in Canada."

Eustacia stood motionless. "How long has he known this?" she asked.

"Well, he knew it early this morning because I heard it from Charlie at ten o'clock. Wildeve's a lucky man. How's Clym?"

"He's well."

"This is a good thing for his cousin. Do you need any assistance? What's mine is yours, you know."

"Thank you, Grandfather. We don't need anything at present," she said.

"Very well. Good night." Captain Vye drove on.

Eustacia walked on mechanically. Eleven thousand pounds! Damon was rich. "He wishes he had me now, so that he could give me everything that I desire," she thought. She sat down on a large rock.

"Eustacia!"

It was Damon. She remained sitting. "What are you doing here? I thought you went home."

"After leaving you, I went to the village. I'm on my way back. Which way are you walking?"

"Toward Blooms End, to meet Clym."

She rose and they walked on together, without speaking, for several minutes.

"I must congratulate you," Eustacia said.

"On my eleven thousand pounds?"

"Yes. Why didn't you tell me when you came today?"

"I felt that to brag of my good fortune would be out of place. Yet, in some ways your husband is a richer man than I am."

"Would you rather have me or your fortune?" she asked with some mischievousness.

"You," he said. "I'll tell you my plans. I'm going to invest nine thousand pounds, keep one thousand as ready money, and, with the remaining thousand, travel for a year or so."

"Where will you go?"

"Paris. Then Italy, Greece, Egypt, and Palestine. In the summer I'll go to America. Then I'll go to Australia and India. Then I'll probably go back to Paris and stay there as long as I can afford to."

"Paris," she murmured in a voice that was

nearly a sigh. "Tamsin will go with you?"

"If she wants to. She might prefer to stay home."

They went on silently for some time. "Haven't you come out of your way, Damon?"

"I'll go with you as far as the hill from which we can see Blooms End."

"I think I'd prefer that you not accompany me any farther. I don't want us to be seen together."

"Very well. I'll leave you." He took her hand and kissed it. "What's that light on the hill?"

She looked and saw a flickering firelight proceeding from the open side of a hut a little way ahead. "Since you've come this far, will you see me safely past that hut?"

When they got near the hut, the firelight and lantern revealed Elizabeth, Clym, and others. Eustacia quickly pulled Damon back from the shed's open side into the shadow. "It's Clym and his mother," she whispered. "Will you find out what's happening?"

Damon moved to the hut's back wall. Presently he beckoned to Eustacia, who joined him. "It's serious," he said. From their position they could overhear.

"I can't think where she was going," Clym said. "Will she be all right?"

The doctor answered, "Exhaustion and heat have overpowered her. Her walk must have been exceptionally long. I believe she's had a stroke."

"Come quickly!" Tamsin cried from the other end of the shed.

Clym and the doctor hurried back to Elizabeth, who gasped and then was silent.

"It's over," the doctor said. "She's dead."

Clym sobbed.

"I must go to Clym," Eustacia said. "But do I dare?"

"No. Come away," Damon said.

When they had withdrawn from the area of the shed, Eustacia said, "I'm to blame for this. There's evil in store for me."

"Wasn't she admitted to your house?" Damon asked.

"No! Clym didn't wake up, so no one let her in. Damon, goodbye! I can't speak to you anymore now."

They parted. When Eustacia reached the next hill, she looked back. A mournful procession was making its way, by lantern light, from the hut to Blooms End.

CHAPTER 15

On a moonlit night three weeks after Elizabeth's funeral, Eustacia was leaning against the garden gate when Humphrey came up the road.

With some hesitation, he asked, "How is Mr. Yeobright tonight, ma'am?"

"Better but still unwell, Humphrey."

"Does he still rave about his mother?"

"Yes, but not as wildly."

Humphrey went away, and Eustacia went inside and up to the front bedroom, where a shaded light was burning.

Clym lay in the bed. He was pale and haggard. "Is it you, Eustacia?"

"Yes, Clym." She sat down.

"Eustacia, my thoughts cut through me like swords. I can't help feeling that I killed her. My conduct toward her was hideous. I never visited her. It was my duty to go and see her. When I finally went, it was too late. Too late!"

"You must stop giving in to despair," Eustacia said. "Other men have lost their mothers."

"That doesn't make the loss of mine any less. I sinned against her."

"She sinned against *you*." Whenever Clym was in this state, Eustacia was haunted by the memory of his mother knocking at the door and not being admitted.

The maid announced that Tamsin had come.

"Tamsin!" Clym said when she entered the room. "Thank you for coming. I'm overcome with remorse. My mother lived alone the last two-and-a-half months of her life. I never went to see her. I wish I were dead!"

"Hush, Clym," Tamsin said gently. "Don't say such things."

"She died on the heath like a wounded, abandoned dog."

"Clym, stop tormenting yourself," Tamsin said.

After a pause, Clym asked, "How long are you going to stay at the inn, now that Damon has inherited all this money?"

"Probably another month or two, until I've given birth."

"How did you get here tonight, Tamsin?" Eustacia asked.

"Damon set me down at the end of the lane. He's driven to East Egdon on business. He'll pick me up soon."

Some time later they heard the sound of wheels. Damon was outside with his horse and carriage. "Please have your servant tell Damon that I'll be down in a few minutes," Tamsin said to Eustacia.

"I'll go down myself," Eustacia said.

Damon stood in front of the horse. As soon as he saw Eustacia, he asked softly, "Did you tell him about his mother's visit?"

"Not yet," Eustacia whispered.

"Wait until he's well, and don't tell him that I was here that day."

Eustacia burst into tears. "Oh, Damon, I'm so unhappy!"

Visibly affected by her distress, Damon took her hand. "You've done nothing to deserve this. I'm most to blame."

"No, *I* am. I'd better go back in. Tamsin says that she'll be down in a few minutes. Goodbye."

CHAPTER 16

A month after Tamsin's visit, Clym's grief had worn itself out. One evening when he was standing in the garden, Christian came up to him. "Mr. Clym, Mr. Wildeve has sent me to tell you that Mrs. Wildeve gave birth to a girl this afternoon."

"Is Mrs. Wildeve well?"

"Yes, sir."

"And the baby?"

"Yes, sir, although Mr. Wildeve is annoyed that the baby isn't a boy."

"Christian, did you see my mother the day that she died?"

"Yes, sir. I saw her before she came here."

"Here?" Clym exclaimed with intense surprise. "Why didn't you ever mention this?"

"I haven't seen you lately, and I didn't think it mattered."

"Did she say why she was coming?"

"Not to me, but she might have told Diggory Venn. He visited her the evening before she set out to see you."

"I must see him. I wish I'd known this before," Clym said. "Christian, will you find Venn and tell him that I wish to see him?"

"Yes, sir."

The next day, Christian searched for Diggory but had no word of him. Clym asked Christian to keep trying.

The day after, Clym set out for his mother's house, which he now owned. It was early afternoon when he reached the valley. He unlocked the garden gate, entered the house, and threw open the shutters. He began going through the cupboards and closets in preparation for his moving in with Eustacia. He noticed that some flowers in the window had died from lack of water. Someone knocked at the door.

Clym opened it and saw Diggory.

"Good morning," Diggory said, "Is Mrs. Yeobright at home?"

Clym looked down. "Then, you don't know."

"I've only just returned after a long stay away," Diggory said.

"My mother is . . . dead."

"Dead!"

"Her home is now my home."

Diggory looked at him. "Have you been ill?"

"Yes. But come in. I've been wanting to see you." Clym led Diggory into the large room in which the Christmas party had taken place. They sat down together.

"How did Mrs. Yeobright come to die?" Diggory asked.

Clym told Diggory as much as he knew. "What did you and my mother talk about when you last saw her?"

"About you. She said she would go to see you."

"She forgave me, then?"

"She didn't blame you at all. She blamed only herself. She told me that. She forgave your wife, too. She was going to see you so that you all could be reconciled."

When Diggory left soon after, Clym was in a state of wonder. That night, he stayed at Blooms End. He barely slept, thinking over the news that his mother had come to see him.

The next day he walked home, determined to ask Eustacia if she had seen his mother the day that she died. When he arrived, the blinds of Eustacia's bedroom still were closed because she was a late riser. Clym entered the cottage and went straight up to Eustacia's room. When he opened the door, she was standing before the mirror in her nightgown, wrapping her mass of black hair around her head.

When Eustacia saw Clym's face in the mirror, she froze. His face was ashy, haggard, and terrible. She paled.

"You know what I'm thinking, don't you?" he said huskily. "I can see it in your face."

She didn't speak.

"Answer me," he ordered. "Did you keep our door shut against my mother the day that she died?"

Eustacia remained silent.

Clym grabbed her by the arm.

"What are you going to do?" she asked with some defiance. "You don't frighten me."

Instead of letting go, Clym pulled her closer. "Tell me about my mother's death," he said in a hard, panting whisper, "or I'll . . ."

"Clym, listen before you hit me."

"Is that what you think? That I'll hit you?"

"I think you might kill me. Your rage against me will match your grief for your mother."

"I won't kill you," he said contemptuously.

"I almost wish that you would," Eustacia said with gloomy bitterness. "I'm tired of the part I've had to play lately. You're no blessing, my husband."

"Did my mother come and you refused to let her in?" he demanded.

"I didn't let her in," Eustacia said softly, "but it wasn't because I refused to. It was because . . ."

"There was someone here with you, wasn't there? A man! You had a man with you, and you couldn't let my mother find out!"

"Go ahead and think your ugly thoughts."

"Tell me his name!"

"I won't."

"Where does he meet you? How often does

he write to you?" Clym looked at Eustacia's small writing desk. He went over to it. It was locked.

"Unlock this!"

"I won't!"

Clym picked up the desk and threw it to the floor. The hinge burst open, and a number of letters tumbled out.

"Stop!" Eustacia cried.

Clym gathered up the letters and examined them. All seemed innocent. But then he noticed an empty envelope addressed to Eustacia. "It seems my lady is well-skilled at a certain trade."

Eustacia gasped. "You say that to me?"

Clym searched further but found nothing more. "What was in the letter?"

"After this, I wouldn't tell you if I were as innocent as the sweetest babe in heaven!"

"Which you aren't."

"I haven't done what you suppose."

"Whether or not you have a lover, you caused my mother's death! Who was with you when my mother came? Was it Damon? Was it poor Tamsin's husband? Why didn't you kick him out and let my mother in? Well, you can't insult her anymore."

"You exaggerate fearfully," she said in a faint, weary voice. "From now on, you're nothing to me. Because of you, I've lost everything, but I haven't complained. Your blunders and misfortunes may have been a sorrow to you, but they've been a wrong to me. Is this how you cherish me? By putting me in a hut and making me the wife of a gorse-cutter? You deceived me, not by words but by appearances."

"What do you mean? Am I the cause of your sin?"

Trembling, Eustacia reached out her hand to Clym. She started to cry.

"Can you shed tears and offer me your hand?"

Eustacia dropped her hand limply, but she continued to cry.

"I wasted foolish kisses on that hand before I knew what you really are. I was bewitched! Everyone spoke ill of you, but I wouldn't listen."

Sobbing, Eustacia sank to her knees. "The first time that your mother knocked, I didn't open the door, but I would have opened it the second time that she knocked if I hadn't thought that you had gone to it yourself. That's the extent of my crime toward her."

"Is Damon the man who was with you?"

"I can't tell," she said through her sobbing. "I'm leaving this house."

"You can stay. I'll go."

"No, I'll go."

"Where?"

"Where I came from or somewhere else."

Eustacia hastily dressed while Clym paced the room. Her hands shook so much that she couldn't tie her bonnet.

Seeing this, Clym moved forward and said, "Let me tie it."

Eustacia lifted her chin and let him tie the bonnet.

"If you'll tell me the name of the man, I may pity you."

Eustacia flung her shawl around her and went downstairs.

Clym remained standing in the room. Soon there was a knock at the bedroom door. "Yes?"

The maid said, "Someone from Mrs. Wildeve's has called to say that Mrs. Wildeve and the baby are doing well and that the baby has been named Eustacia Clementine."

CHAPTER 17

Eustacia went to her grandfather's house. Finding the front door locked, she went to the stable. Charlie was there. "Captain Vye isn't home?" she asked.

"No, ma'am. He went to Weatherbury. He won't be home until later. The house is locked."

Eustacia had a wild, forlorn look.

"Can I help you, ma'am?"

"I wish I could get into the house."

"I'll try to open the door," Charlie said. He climbed in through a back window and opened the door. "Shall I get you something to eat and drink?" he asked Eustacia.

"Yes, please."

Charlie returned with tea and toast on a tray. Eustacia sat on the couch and sipped some tea, but she couldn't eat. She went upstairs to lie down.

Later in the afternoon her grandfather returned. He was about to question her when he saw how bad she looked.

"Yes, it's too bad for words," she said in

response to his glance. "Can my old room be gotten ready for me tonight, Grandfather?"

Captain Vye ordered that the room be prepared.

For a week Eustacia never left the house. Then she took to looking out over the heath through her grandfather's telescope. One day she saw a wagon where the highroad crossed the distant valley. It was piled with household furniture. She looked again and recognized it as her own. In the evening her grandfather came indoors and reported that Clym had moved, that day, from Alderworth to Blooms End.

When Eustacia looked through the telescope on another day, she saw Tamsin and her maid Rachel walking in the valley. Tamsin held her baby daughter in her arms.

On Guy Fawkes Day, thinking to please Eustacia, Charlie lit a bonfire precisely where Eustacia had lit one the past two years. Because the house was shuttered, Eustacia didn't notice the bonfire for quite a while. Then Charlie sent word that she should open the shutters. As soon as Eustacia saw the bonfire, she put on her bonnet and cloak and went outside, fearing that Damon would see the fire and regard it as a signal inviting him to come. Before she could ask Charlie to put it out, Damon stood before her.

"I didn't light it!" Eustacia said quickly. "It was lit without my knowledge. Don't come over to me!"

"Why have you been living here all these days without telling me? You've left your husband. Am I the reason?"

"He discovered that I didn't let his mother in."

"You don't deserve such treatment. I can see how unhappy you are."

Eustacia reacted to this sympathy by bursting into sobs. Ashamed, she turned aside.

Damon resisted the impulse to embrace her and stood without speaking. "It makes me sad to see you this way," he said with emotion and deference.

"I didn't send for you, Damon. I'm in pain, but I didn't send for you. I've been a faithful wife."

"Never mind. I'm here. Eustacia, forgive me for the harm that I've caused you. I've been your ruin."

"Not you. This place."

"No, I'm to blame. I should have left you alone or married you. Can I do anything to help you? I'm rich now. Do you want anything that can be bought? Do you want to go anywhere?"

"We're each married to someone else. I can't accept assistance from you."

"I know my duty to Tamsin as well as I know my duty to you as a woman I have wronged. How can I help you?"

"Help me get away from here."

"Where do you want to go?"

"If you can help me get to Budmouth, I'll take a steamer from there to France. I want to go to Paris. Help me get to Budmouth without my grandfather or husband finding out, and I can do the rest."

"Will it be safe to leave you there alone?"

"Yes. I know Budmouth well."

"Shall I go with you? Say yes, my sweet!"

Eustacia was silent.

"Well, let me know when you want to go. Tamsin and I will be at the inn until December. Then we'll move to Casterbridge. Until then, command me in anything."

"I'll think about this," Eustacia said hurriedly. "I need to consider whether I can accept your help solely as a friend. If I want to go and decide to accept your company, I'll signal to you some evening at eight. That will mean that you should meet me at midnight with a horse and carriage to drive me to Budmouth in time for the morning boat."

"Where should we meet?" Damon asked.

"A quarter of a mile below the inn?"

"Why don't you let me come for you?"

"My grandfather might hear. Besides, it's much longer for someone to drive along the road than for me to walk down to the valley."

"Are you sure?"

"Yes."

"As you wish. I'll look out every night at eight," he said.

"Now please go away. If I decide on this escape, I can meet you only one more time unless I decide that I can't go without you."

Damon slowly walked away, glancing back until Eustacia no longer was visible.

CHAPTER 18

Clym moved into Blooms End. Without pleasure he swept leaves from the garden paths, cut dead stalks from the flower beds, and did other work around the premises. He constantly watched and listened for Eustacia. He hoped that she would return to him. So that she would know where to find him, he'd had a notice of his new address attached to the garden gate at Alderworth. The more he reflected on his treatment of Eustacia, the more he softened toward her. Now that his initial anger had subsided, he didn't believe that she and Damon were lovers. Her manner had suggested otherwise. "Why," he wondered, "hasn't she been open with me?"

The night of Guy Fawkes Day he went to see Tamsin and Damon, but he found only Tamsin at home. As always, Tamsin was glad to see Clym. She took him to see the sleeping baby.

"Tamsin, have you heard that Eustacia and I have separated?" Clym asked.

"No," Tamsin said, alarmed.

"You haven't heard that I've left Alderworth?"

"No. What's happened?"

In a disturbed voice, Clym told her about Eustacia's having failed to let his mother into the house.

"Terrible! How could she do it? When you found out, were you furious? Were you too cruel to Eustacia?"

"Perhaps."

"Do try to be reconciled. Send for her."

"What if she won't come?"

"It will prove her guilty, by showing that she nurses ill will—which I don't believe."

"Is Damon away from home?" Clym asked, suspicious.

"No. He just went out for a walk."

"Why didn't you go with him? It's a lovely evening, and you could use some fresh air."

"I have the baby to look after."

"Yes, of course."

Before going to bed that night, Clym wrote:

My Dear Eustacia,

I must obey my heart more than my reason. Will you come back to me? If you do, I'll never mention the past. I was too severe. I know that you've suffered. Our love must continue. I couldn't ask you back at first because I believed that Damon was your lover. Please come and explain the real circumstances. I'll listen. Return, and I'll welcome you warmly.

Your husband as ever,
Clym

Meanwhile, Tamsin sat alone, uneasy. When Damon returned from his walk, she asked, "Damon, where have you been? I don't like your vanishing in the evenings. There's something on your mind. What is it? You've said that you dislike the heath. Then, why do you walk there so much?"

Disconcerted, Damon sat down.

"I've heard talk that you used to see Eustacia in the evenings. I've heard that you used to be very fond of her."

"Well, there's nothing new in that," he said. "Let's not talk about it."

CHAPTER 19

The next day, toward evening, Eustacia packed a bundle of her things. At eight o'clock she lit a fire as the signal to Damon. Then she returned to her room to wait for midnight.

Captain Vye sat downstairs sipping rum. Around ten o'clock, Timothy Fairway knocked on the door. "Mr. Yeobright asked me to bring this letter," he said, handing it to Captain Vye, and he left.

Seeing that the letter was addressed to Eustacia, Captain Vye brought it up to her room. The room was dark, so he believed that Eustacia was asleep. In fact, she was awake but resting on the bed. Rather than disturb her, Captain Vye placed the letter on the mantelpiece to give her in the morning.

Shortly before midnight, Eustacia set out into the darkness. It was raining. Sometimes stumbling, she headed toward the meeting place. Suddenly she realized that she didn't have enough money for a long journey. To ask Damon for financial assistance without allowing him to accompany her was impossible to a woman with any pride. To flee as his lover would be a humiliation. "How can I go?" she moaned. "He isn't great enough for me to love," she thought. "He's not worth my breaking my marriage vow. But I have no money to go alone." The rain had become a storm. Eustacia stood in the downpour, despairing. Every thought of her future was bleak. Simply being alive was painful.

Clym, meanwhile, anxiously awaited some response to his letter. Around 10:30, despite his anxiety, he went to bed and fell asleep. Around an hour later, someone knocked at his door.

"Oh, Clym, come down and let me in!" It was Tamsin.

Clym hurried down and let Tamsin in. She was wet, frightened, and panting. "Has Eustacia come home to you?"

"No."

"I think that she and Damon are planning to run off together! Tonight about eight, Damon said in an offhanded way, 'Tamsie, I've just found out that I must go on a journey.' 'When?' I said. 'Tonight,' he said. 'Where?' I said. 'I can't tell you now,' he said. 'I'll be back tomorrow.' Then he gathered some things. He took no notice of me at all. I expected him to leave at once, but he didn't. At ten he said, 'You'd better go to bed.' I went to my bedroom but didn't fall asleep. I heard him unlock the oak chest in which we keep money. After a while I heard him in the stable. I think he's been meeting with Eustacia in the evenings! I think they're going to run away together! I didn't know what to do, so I slipped out and came to you. Please try to keep him from going, Clym!"

"I'll try," Clym said. He ran upstairs to dress. When he came back down, he said, "Tamsin, dry yourself. I'll do what I can." And he left the house.

Soon after, finding that she couldn't sit and do nothing, Tamsin ventured back out into the storm and headed to the inn. Distracted by worry, she lost her way. Before long she spotted Diggory's wagon. When she approached it, Diggory was startled.

"Mrs. Wildeve!" he exclaimed. "What are you doing out here?" Taking her by the arm, he pulled her into the shelter of his wagon.

"I've lost my way coming from Blooms End. I'm in a hurry to get home. Please show me the path, Diggory."

"Of course. I'll go with you." Diggory locked his wagon.

Tamsin followed him as he wound right and left to avoid bushes. "How far are we from the inn?" she asked.

"About a quarter of a mile."

"Can we go faster?"

"I was afraid you wouldn't be able to keep up," Diggory said.

"I'm anxious to get there."

CHAPTER 20

At 11:40 Damon quietly harnessed his horse and led him, with the carriage, to the prearranged meeting place about a quarter of a mile below the inn. Damon waited there. He had decided to give Tamsin half of his property and spend the rest of his life with Eustacia.

At a quarter past midnight, Damon started wondering if Eustacia had decided not to venture out in the storm. He wished that he had insisted on driving to her grandfather's house.

Damon heard footsteps. "Eustacia?"

Clym stepped forward into the light of Damon's lantern.

Both men now heard the sound of someone falling into a nearby stream.

"Good God!" Clym exclaimed. "Take one of the lamps, and come with me."

Damon followed Clym to the stream. They saw a dark form floating on the current.

"Oh, my darling!" Damon cried. He leaped in.

Clym, too, sprang in.

Tamsin and Diggory now reached the horse and carriage and saw the lantern that Clym had placed beside the water. Diggory observed something floating motionless. "Mrs. Wildeve, run home," Diggory said hastily. "Call the stable boy, and have him send men. Someone has fallen into the stream."

Tamsin ran to the inn. She woke the stable boy and ran out to give the alarm at the nearest cottage.

Holding his lantern aloft, Diggory entered the stream. He saw a woman's bonnet floating alone. Then something else came to the surface. To Diggory's surprise, it was a man, not a woman. Diggory took the lantern's ring in his teeth and seized the floating man by his collar. He and the unconscious man were carried downstream. As soon as Diggory found his feet dragging over the pebbles of the stream's shallower part, he secured his footing and waded toward the bank. There, where the water was waist high, he attempted to drag the man out. But he found that the man's legs were embraced by another man, who had been entirely beneath the surface until now.

Two men, sent by Tamsin, now ran to Diggory and helped him lift the two bodies out of the water, separate them, and lay them on the grass. Diggory turned the light onto their faces.

One was Clym; the other, Damon.

"We must search," Diggory said. "A woman is in here somewhere. Get a pole."

One of the men ran to a footbridge and tore off a handrail. Diggory and the two men then entered the water and probed it. After a while, something impeded their thrust. "Pull it forward," Diggory said. They raked it in with the pole. Diggory vanished under the stream and came up with Eustacia's cold body.

When they reached the bank, Tamsin was bending over the forms of Clym and Damon. The carriage was brought to the nearest point in the road, and the bodies of Eustacia, Clym, and Damon were placed inside. Diggory led the horse while supporting Tamsin on his arm.

At the inn the bodies were brought inside and laid on the carpet. The stable boy went to fetch a doctor.

Tamsin held smelling salts to Damon's nostrils. There was no response. She did the same with Clym. He noticeably breathed. "Clym's alive!" she exclaimed. Again and again, Tamsin tried to revive Damon, but he showed no sign of life.

When the doctor arrived, he said that Eustacia and Damon were dead. Clym was carried upstairs to bed. The doctor instructed that Tamsin, too, be put into a warm bed. The bodies of Eustacia and Damon also were brought upstairs.

After a time, a servant came downstairs holding a rolled mass of wet paper. She took some string from a cupboard, tied it like a clothesline across the fireplace, and, unrolling the wet papers, began pinning them one by one to the string.

"What's that?" Diggory asked.

"Poor master's banknotes," she answered. "They were found in his pocket when they undressed him."

Diggory retired into a niche of the fireplace. From there he watched the steam from the row of banknotes as they waved backward and forward in the chimney draft until their limpness changed to crispness. Then the servant unpinned them and, folding them together, carried the handful upstairs.

Presently the doctor came down and, with the look of a man who can do no more, put on his gloves and left.

CHAPTER 21

The story of Eustacia's and Damon's deaths was told throughout Egdon, and far beyond, for many months. Tamsin grieved for her dead husband but focused on her living daughter. Spring came and calmed her. Summer came and soothed her. Her little girl was strong and happy, growing in size and knowledge every day.

Tamsin inherited all of Damon's wealth, but she chose to live at Blooms End. Clym occupied two rooms at the top of the back staircase, while Tamsin and little Eustacia occupied the rest of the house, along with three servants.

For a man of Clym's simple habits, the house and the 120 pounds a year that he had inherited from his mother sufficed to supply all worldly needs. Largely, he went his own way and thought his own thoughts. Grief had aged him, but inwardly. It could be said that he had a wrinkled mind. He had no enemies. No one blamed him. But he bitterly blamed himself. As with his mother, he blamed himself for not having forgiven

Eustacia sooner. He frequently walked alone on the heath.

Winter returned, with its winds, frosts, and sparkling starlight. Clym read books of exceptionally large type. He shared the life of Tamsin, little Eustacia, and the servants only insofar as he overheard them. He would hear Tamsin rocking the cradle; Tamsin humming Eustacia to sleep; Humphrey, Timothy, or Sam walking across the kitchen's stone floor. Despite her new wealth, Tamsin led a simple, narrow life. She saved every possible pound for little Eustacia.

One summer day, Diggory came to visit Tamsin. Upon seeing him, she gave a slight scream and exclaimed, "Oh, how you frightened me!"

No longer a ruddleman, Diggory looked like a gentleman. He wore a white shirt, flower-patterned waistcoat, blue-spotted neckerchief, and bottle-green coat. There was no red in either his skin or his clothing. "I gave up dealing in ruddle last Christmas," Diggory said. "I've taken over the fifty-cow dairy that belonged to my father."

"You look much better than ever before," Tamsin said. Then she blushed slightly. "Sit down, Diggory, and stay to tea."

Diggory moved toward the kitchen.

"No," Tamsin said with playful pertness, "you must sit here with me. Where is your dairy?"

"At Stickleford, about two miles east of Alderworth, where the meadow begins. Mr.

Yeobright is welcome to pay me a visit any time. I can't stay to tea this afternoon, thank you, because I have some business that must be settled." Diggory soon left.

On May Day, eighteen months after the deaths of Eustacia and Damon, a Maypole was erected in the middle of a green near Blooms End. It was adorned with flowers whose perfume spread into the surrounding air. At the top of the pole were crossed hoops decorated with small flowers. Beneath these were other flowers, including bluebells, lilacs, and daffodils. Tamsin was delighted that the Maypole dancing would be right by the house.

In the afternoon people began to gather on the green. Clym looked out at them from his window. Soon after, he saw Tamsin walk outside directly below. She was dressed more gaily than she had been since her wedding day.

"You look very pretty today, Tamsin," he said, "Are you dressed up because of May Day?"

"Not entirely." She blushed and dropped her eyes.

Clym wondered if Tamsin had dressed up to please *him*. Over the last few weeks, they had spent much time working together in the garden. Had Tamsin developed a romantic interest in him? He felt no sexual passion for Tamsin, as he had felt for Eustacia. But he was very fond of her and found her attractive.

About five o'clock a brass band arrived and started playing. To avoid the noise of the festivities and think further about his relationship to Tamsin, Clym left the house. For several hours, he pondered whether or not he and Tamsin should marry. It was a shame for such a sweet, young, and appealing woman to be without a mate. Also, his mother had desired the marriage. Shouldn't he, at last, fulfill her wish? On the other hand, what kind of husband would he be? Didn't Tamsin deserve a more cheerful, loving companion? Still, he leaned toward proposing to her.

When Clym returned to the house, the music had ceased. He saw Tamsin alone on the porch. She looked at him reproachfully. "You went away just when it began, Clym."

"Yes, I didn't feel that I could join in. *You* joined in, didn't you?"

"No."

"I thought that you dressed up in order to join in."

"I did. But I was embarrassed to go alone. Now everyone has left except for Diggory."

Clym looked out and noticed Diggory on the green. "Why didn't you ask him to come in? He's always been extremely kind to you."

"I'll ask him now," Tamsin said. Going up to Diggory, she asked, "Diggory, will you come in?"

"I'm afraid that I . . ."

"I saw you dancing this evening. You had the finest young women for your partners."

Clym's face became grave.

"You don't like him!" Tamsin exclaimed with disappointment.

"I do like him," Clym said. "He's an honest, clever man. But really, Tamsin, he isn't quite . . ."

"Quite enough of a gentleman? That's what I thought. At the same time, I won't marry anyone else."

"Why not? You could marry a professional man by going into the town to live and forming acquaintances there."

"I'm not suited to town life. I'm rural through and through. I couldn't live on a paved street for all the world. I couldn't be happy anywhere but Egdon."

"Neither could I," Clym said.

"Then, how can you say that I should marry some town man? I'm sure that I'll marry Diggory or no one. He's been kinder to me than anyone else and has helped me in many ways." Tamsin almost pouted now.

"Yes, he has," Clym said. "I wish with all my heart that I could say 'Marry him,' but I can't forget what my mother thought, and I want to respect her opinion."

"Very well," Tamsin sighed. "I won't say any more."

"You aren't bound to obey my wishes. I'm only stating my opinion."

"I don't want to be rebellious," she said sadly.

"I'm waiting for the moon to rise."

"To see how pretty the Maypole looks in the moonlight?"

"No. To look for a glove that one of the maidens dropped."

Tamsin was speechless with surprise. Although Diggory had to walk four or five miles to his home, he was waiting to find a glove? He must be in love with the glove's owner! "Were you dancing with her, Diggory?" Tamsin asked with keen interest.

"No," he sighed.

"You won't come in, then?"

"Not tonight. Thank you, ma'am."

"Shall I lend you a lantern to look for the young lady's glove?"

"That won't be necessary, Mrs. Wildeve. Thank you. The moon will rise in a few minutes."

Tamsin returned to the porch.

"Is he coming in?" Clym said.

"Not tonight," she said. Then she and Clym retired to their rooms.

After a little while, Tamsin crept upstairs in the dark, went to the window, gently lifted the corner of the white curtain, and looked out. Diggory still was there. She watched the moon suddenly flood the green with light. Diggory bent down and searched the grass for the missing glove.

Annoyed, Tamsin thought, "How ridiculous! To think that he—a respectable dairyman and a man of money—should be silly enough to moon around like that for a woman's glove!"

Diggory now found the glove. He stood, kissed it, and placed it in his breast pocket. Then he headed home.

For several days Clym saw little of Tamsin. When they met, she was quieter than usual. "What are you thinking about so intently?" he asked.

"I'm completely puzzled," she said candidly. "Diggory is in love with someone, and I can't think who it is. None of the girls at the Maypole was good enough for him, yet she must have been there."

Clym could offer no enlightenment.

One afternoon Tamsin was upstairs getting ready for a walk when she failed to find one of her gloves. Holding up a glove, she asked her thirteen-year-old servant, "Rachel, have you seen the match to this glove?"

Rachel didn't answer.

"Why don't you answer?" Tamsin said.

"I think it's lost, ma'am."

"Lost? Who lost it?"

Rachel began to cry. "Please, ma'am. On May Day I didn't have any gloves to wear, and I saw yours on the table. I thought I'd borrow them. I didn't mean any harm, but I lost one of them. Someone gave me money to buy another pair for you, but I haven't been able to go anywhere to get them."

"Who gave you money?"

"Mr. Venn."

"Did he know it was my glove?"

"Yes. I told him."

Tamsin was so surprised by the explanat that she forgot to scold Rachel, who glided aw

The next day, Tamsin was walking on heath with little Eustacia when Diggory came on horseback. He waved his hat and bowed lantly.

"Diggory, give me my glove," Tamsin sa

Diggory immediately dismounted, read into his breast pocket, and handed over the gl

"Thank you. It was very good of you to care of it."

After some pleasant conversation, Dig remounted and rode on.

One evening two months later, Clym d ed that the time had come for him to propo Tamsin. He had a pleasant sense of fulfillin duty. "For a long time, I've wanted to talk a our futures, Tamsin," he said.

"I've been wanting to talk, too," Tamsin eagerly. "I'm thinking of marrying, but I your approval."

Clym was silent.

"Why don't you speak?"

"I was taken by surprise. But I'm very gl hear such news. Who's the lucky man?"

"Diggory Venn."

"I had no business to think of him." Her lips trembled, and she turned away to hide a tear.

The next few days, Tamsin moped around the garden. Clym was half-angry with her for choosing Diggory. On the other hand, he felt guilty about being an obstacle to her happiness and Diggory's. Diggory was as honest and persevering as anyone he'd ever met.

At their next meeting, Tamsin abruptly said, "Diggory is much more respectable now than he was before! Aunt objected only because he was a ruddleman."

"Well, perhaps I don't know all the particulars of my mother's wishes. You'd better use your own judgment."

"You'll always feel that I slighted your mother's memory."

"No, I won't. I'll think that you're convinced that, had she seen Diggory in his present position, she would have considered him a fitting husband for you. That's my real feeling. Do as you like, Tamsin, and I'll be content."

A few days later, when Clym strayed into a part of the heath that he hadn't visited lately, Humphrey, who was working there, said to him, "I'm glad to see that Mrs. Wildeve and Mr. Venn have made it up."

As Clym descended into the valley, Tamsin came down by the other path and met him at the gate. "What do you think I have to tell you,

Clym?" she said.

"I can guess," he replied.

She examined his face. "Yes, you guess right. If you don't object, Diggory and I will be married on the twenty-fifth of next month."

"Do what you think is right, dear. I'm glad that you've found happiness."

CHAPTER 22

After their wedding ceremony, Tamsin and Diggory returned to Egdon in an open carriage, with Clym and a relative of Diggory's. The carriage had been hired at the nearest town, regardless of cost, because in Diggory's opinion nothing in Egdon was too dignified for a bride such as Tamsin.

Having given the bride away and then returned to Blooms End with the bride and groom, Clym didn't want to join in the feasting and dancing that would wind up the evening. Tamsin was disappointed.

"I wish I could be there," Clym said, "but I'd only lower everyone's spirits. I know it seems unkind, but I really wouldn't be comfortable. I'll come often to see you at your new home, so my absence now won't matter."

"Then, I give in," Tamsin said. "Do whatever is most comfortable for you."

Relieved, Clym retired to his rooms upstairs. During the afternoon, he made notes for what would be his first sermon. He had decided to become a traveling preacher. His eyesight had improved but not enough for him to return to his original plan of becoming a schoolmaster.

With evening, the sounds of life and movement in the lower part of the house became more pronounced. The outside gate repeatedly clicked open and shut. Clym heard merriment and singing.

Finally, after all the guests had gone, Diggory and Tamsin were ready to leave for Diggory's farm in Stickleford. Diggory's handyman arrived in a four-wheeled cart, and Tamsin and Diggory took their seats. Holding little Eustacia, Rachel sat behind on the open flap.

Tamsin bent down to wish Clym good night. "Now we leave you in absolute possession of your house. I hope you won't be lonely."

Clym smiled sadly, and the group drove off. Back inside, the only sound was the ticking of the clock. Clym sat and remained in thought a long time. Mostly, he thought of his mother. She had been right in advising him not to marry Eustacia, who had paid dearly for his poor judgment. "It was all my fault," he whispered.

The Sunday afternoon after the wedding, Clym stood atop Rainbarrow, preaching. Many people sat and reclined around him, listening. This was the first of a series of sermons that Clym would deliver every Sunday until the weather turned cold. Now thirty-three, he wore a shade over his eyes. His face was pensive and lined, but his voice was rich and stirring, even musical. "My talks," he said, "will sometimes be religious, sometimes not. My texts will come from all kinds of books." Clym had found his calling.

From that day on, Clym labored ceaselessly. He spoke not only at Rainbarrow but also in neighboring towns and villages: in barns, town halls, and market squares; on bridges, wharves, and seaside walkways. He preached simple, universal truths. Some found wisdom in his words; others did not. But everyone treated him kindly because the story of his life was widely known.

AFTERWORD

ABOUT THE AUTHOR

In many ways Thomas Hardy resembled his character Clym Yeobright. Like Clym, he lived most of his life in rural southwest England. He was born, in 1840, in a cottage in Higher Bockhampton, a village in Dorset County, the setting of *The Return of the Native.*

Like the Yeobright cottage, the cottage in which Hardy grew up overlooked a heath. "I love the heath," Clym says. "I find it exhilarating, strengthening, and soothing. I'd rather live here than anywhere else in the world." Hardy felt the same way. He lived in the family cottage until he was thirty-four and spent most of the rest of his life nearby.

Hardy's father was a builder. After being apprenticed to a local architect at age sixteen, Hardy first supported himself as a builder and architect. For some years, Clym works in Paris for a diamond company; then he returns to his native locale. Similarly, from 1862 to 1867 Hardy worked in London as an architect; then he returned home. Like Clym, Hardy read and wrote in an upstairs room of the family cottage.

Hardy resembled Clym in his personal relationships as well. By his own admission, Hardy modeled Clym's mother after his own: Jemima Hardy, who lived in the Dorset cottage until her death. Domineering and possessive, Jemima demanded devotion from her two sons and two daughters. She could be cold and sarcastic and had a disapproving nature. Still, Hardy grieved when she died, just as Clym mourns *his* possessive, disapproving mother.

Clym is fond of his cousin Tamsin Yeobright and considers marrying her. When Hardy returned to Dorset in 1867, he often met privately with his cousin Tryphena Sparks. The extent to which the relationship was sexual isn't known, but Hardy and Tryphena apparently became engaged. In *The Return of the Native*, Hardy repeatedly describes Tamsin as "sweet." In a poem written years later, Hardy used the same word for Tryphena. But Hardy, again like Clym, ultimately chose a more fiery woman: Emma Gifford. Hardy and Emma fell in love in 1870. Two years later, Hardy and Tryphena ended their engagement. Tamsin says of Clym, "He loved me once." Tryphena may well have said the same of Hardy. In 1877 Tryphena married the owner of an inn, as Tamsin does. *The Return of the Native* was published the next year.

By this time, Hardy was married to Emma. The wedding had taken place in 1874, the same year that Hardy's *Far from the Madding Crowd* was published. The novel's success had enabled Hardy to give up architecture and devote himself full-time to writing. Similarly, when Clym comes into his inheritance, he turns to penning sermons.

Hardy's wife seems to have inspired the character of Eustacia Vye, who is willful, proud, and sexually enticing. Before meeting Clym, Eustacia daydreams about him. Egdon's residents discuss his scheduled return with much anticipation. Emma and others in her village awaited Hardy, who had been hired to restore the village church, with equal eagerness. When Eustacia first meets Clym, she is struck by his voice; Emma was struck by Hardy's. Clym admires Eustacia's arresting eyes and luxuriant hair; Hardy admired Emma's. Like Clym and Eustacia, Hardy and Emma were immediately smitten with each other. The real-life marriage followed the same basic course as the fictional one: passionate and blissfully happy, then unhappy. Eustacia haughtily says that she "condescended" to marry Clym. Apparently, Emma frequently reminded Hardy that her social class outranked his.

Elizabeth Yeobright objects to her son's marriage and doesn't get along with her daughter-in-law. The same was true of Hardy's mother. Hardy may have come to regret that he didn't marry

Tryphena. Over the years, he formed intense attachments (perhaps sexual) with a succession of women. Increasingly he and Emma spent time apart. They never had children.

In 1912 Emma suddenly died. Like Clym after Eustacia's death, Hardy grieved and felt guilty about not having shown his wife more kindness and understanding. In 1914 Hardy married his secretary, Florence Dugdale. He was 73; she was 35.

When Hardy died at age 87 in 1928, he was the world-famous author of such novels as *The Mayor of Casterbridge* (1886), *Tess of the d'Urbervilles* (1891), and *Jude the Obscure* (1896). He also had published three short-story collections and more than 900 poems. In many of his works he explored the failure of personal relationships, especially romantic ones, similar to those in his own life.

ABOUT THE BOOK

The Return of the Native (1878) is filled with concealment, which has tragic results. People spy and eavesdrop on one another. They hide, disguise themselves, and meet in secret. They withhold important information and outright lie. The consequences include three deaths.

The book opens at twilight, when the people on Egdon Heath are becoming increasingly invisible. The first character we meet—Diggory Venn—is partially disguised by his skin's red tint, acquired through continual contact with ruddle, a red iron ore. Because of Diggory's redness, Humphrey Miller doesn't recognize him: "I think I've seen him before." Similarly, Elizabeth Yeobright doesn't immediately recognize Diggory.

Although Diggory likes to remain unseen, he closely watches others. "His blue eyes were as keen as a bird of prey's." He's far more eager to obtain information than to provide it. When Captain Vye asks him who is inside his wagon, Diggory won't say. "May I look at her?" Vye asks. "No," Diggory answers sharply. "Why did you become a ruddleman?" Elizabeth asks Diggory. He changes the subject.

Despite her "honest" face, Tamsin Yeobright also continually conceals. She doesn't tell her aunt that Diggory once proposed to her. After her wedding to Damon Wildeve is postponed, she tries to hide that fact. So do Damon Wildeve and Elizabeth. When villagers come to congratulate Tamsin and Damon on their wedding, Elizabeth cries, "Tamsin, here's a pretty exposure! We must leave at once." Before Damon has finished talking to the visitors, Tamsin and Elizabeth leave through a back window. Instead of informing the well-wishers that the wedding has been postponed, Damon accepts their congratulations. Tamsin and Elizabeth conceal the incident from Clym.

Eustacia Vye and Damon meet in secret, and Diggory spies on them. "Each of the next five nights, Diggory went to Rainbarrow to eavesdrop on Eustacia and Damon, but they didn't come. On the sixth night, he saw them at the barrow. He crawled near enough to overhear." Speaking of Damon, Diggory says to Eustacia, "I think that he occasionally meets this other woman on the heath." In truth, Diggory knows that Damon meets Eustacia. When Diggory reveals his knowledge, Eustacia is alarmed at having been discovered. She "gasped, and her lips trembled."

Eustacia, too, habitually eavesdrops, spies, and deceives. Using her grandfather's naval telescope, she watches people on the heath. Having kept a bonfire burning as a signal to Damon, she falsely tells her grandfather that she has maintained the fire to please a young boy. Eustacia eavesdrops while Sam Brown and Humphrey discuss Clym's homecoming. In order to attend the Yeobrights' Christmas party, she pretends to be a man playing the part of a knight. Disguised by her costume, she spies on Clym and Tamsin. She soon starts meeting secretly with Clym as she previously met with Damon.

The evening of Clym and Eustacia's wedding, Damon overhears Christian Cantle say that he has something to deliver to Tamsin. "What do you have to deliver?" Damon asks. "It's a secret," Christian replies. Meanwhile, Diggory too is listening in. He has been sitting, "unnoticed," in the chimney corner. Diggory follows Damon and Christian and watches their gambling from behind a bush. When Tamsin receives the hundred guineas, she doesn't tell Damon, who doesn't tell *her* that he attempted to take the money.

At the East Egdon festival, Damon dances with Eustacia. "If you don't want to be recognized, lower your veil," he advises. She does. As Damon and Eustacia are walking home, Diggory and Clym approach. Damon quickly leaves, to avoid being recognized. When Elizabeth comes to Eustacia and Clym's home, Damon leaves by the back door—once again, to avoid being seen. Then Eustacia conceals both Damon's visit and Elizabeth's from Clym. While Elizabeth is dying inside the hut, Damon and Eustacia hide outside, listening. Finally, Eustacia and Damon plan to run off together.

However, Clym may be the most self-concealing character of all. While claiming to love Eustacia "beyond all description," he continually disregards her wishes. Eustacia wants to go to Paris. Clym refuses to take her there. She wants him to stop working as a field laborer. He shrugs off her pleas. When Tamsin seeks his approval regarding her proposed marriage to Diggory, Clym doesn't reveal that he himself had decided to propose to her. He objects to the marriage on the grounds that Diggory is a farmer (so was Clym's own father) and Elizabeth would have disapproved. Readers may well conclude that Clym isn't being fully honest even with himself. "I'm glad that you've found happiness," he tells Tamsin, but the words seem insincere. He can't even bring himself to attend the wedding celebration.

Throughout *The Return of the Native*, Hardy uses concealment as both a plot device and a theme. Concealment creates tension and leads to misunderstandings that cause people to take destructive actions. It also reflects an absence of deep and lasting love, which requires openness and trust.

After Eustacia refuses to acknowledge that Damon came to see her at the cottage, Clym wonders, "Why hasn't she been open with me?" At least in part, the reason is fear. Eustacia dreads Clym's having a bad opinion of her, and her dread is well founded. Based on mere appearances, Clym wrongly concludes that she has committed adultery. Like his mother, he's quick to judge Eustacia harshly. Eustacia feels insecure about Clym's love because his love *is* superficial, more a physical infatuation than an eagerness for her well-being. Perhaps because she senses that Damon doesn't judge her, Eustacia is more open with Damon than she is with Clym. And, ultimately, Damon shows her more tenderness and respect than Clym does. Unlike Clym, Damon tries to help Eustacia and fulfill her wishes.

Compared to Diggory's love for Tamsin—perhaps even Damon's love for Eustacia—Clym's love for Eustacia is shallow and selfish. Whereas Diggory seeks to protect Tamsin and see her happy, Clym shows little actual regard for Eustacia's happiness. Similarly, when he decides to propose to Tamsin, he seems more interested in feeling good about himself than in making Tamsin happy. "He had a pleasant sense of fulfilling his duty," we read. A sense of duty isn't love. At the end of the novel, we believe that Tamsin and Diggory will live without concealment because their household will be filled with love.